CHRISTMAS DOORSTEP ORPHAN

DOLLY PRICE

PUREREAD.COM

Copyright © 2023 PureRead Ltd

www.pureread.com

All rights reserved. No part of this publication may be reproduced, distributed or transmitted in any form or by any means, without prior written permission.

Publisher's Note: This is a work of fiction. Names, characters, places, and incidents are a product of the author's imagination. Locales and public names are sometimes used for atmospheric purposes. Any resemblance to actual people, living or dead, or to businesses, companies, events, institutions, or locales is completely coincidental.

CONTENTS

Dear reader, get ready for another great story… 1
1. CHRISTMAS CHILD 3
2. THE SONS 6
3. CHARLOTTE'S ALARM 11
4. A HOME IS FOUND 14
5. THE MOORES 18
6. BABY WILLIAM 24
7. MONEY DRIES UP 27
8. MILK AND CAKE! 29
9. WHAT WILL BECOME OF HER 36
10. YOU 'AVE 'IS MINCERS! 39
11. THE GIFT 45
12. IN SERVICE 50
13. 'HER OWN PEOPLE' 55
14. THE LETTER 61
15. CHARLOTTE'S SOLUTION 64
16. LEGAL LETTER 66
17. DUDLEY POND 70
18. "FORGET ABOUT THEM EMMA!" 73
19. MR. POND'S WAGER 77
20. A BIG PORKY 86
21. THE ACTOR 92
22. COUSIN MORTIMER 96
23. WHO WINS THE WAGER 98
24. WHERE IS SHE? 105
25. THE FAIRGROVE HOTEL 109
26. THE SEARCH 116
27. THE PARTING 119
28. FOR THE LOVE OF MONEY 124
29. RICH RELATIONS 127
30. VANISHED 135
31. RIVERSEDGE HOUSE 140

32. DR CADOGAN — 147
33. DIAGNOSIS — 153
34. THE FOUL WARD — 157
35. THE PATIENTS — 161
36. CHRISTMAS IN THE LEPERS CAVE — 166
37. PATRICK'S CROSS — 171
38. TWO YEARS LATER — 177
39. MY FATHER IS… — 182
40. THE RELATIONS — 185
41. WHAT HAPPENED ON THE HILL — 189
42. EMMA AND HER FATHER — 194
43. THE NEW WORLD — 198
44. THE FOUNT — 202
45. PATRICK RETURNS — 208
46. NEW WORLD — 210
47. HEARTBREAK AGAIN — 214
48. THE SUFFRAGETTE — 222
49. QUEENSTOWN — 225
50. NEWGATE — 228
51. RIVERSEDGE AGAIN — 231
52. THE PURSUER — 235
53. THE DAGGER — 238
54. TILLY — 242
55. FREEDOM — 250
56. RIVERSEDGE IN RUINS — 256
57. WINDFALL — 259
58. CHRISTMAS CHILD — 261
    Love Victorian Christmas Saga Romance? — 267
    Have You Read — 268

Our Gift To You — 299

DEAR READER, GET READY FOR ANOTHER GREAT STORY...

A VICTORIAN ROMANCE

A Christmas child left on a doorstep, a destitute Whitechapel family tasked with her care, and a web of long-concealed family mysteries that refuse to stay hidden.

Prepare for a heart-stopping romantic saga packed with surprising twists, where every page turned brings you closer to a tearful Christmas miracle that will tug at your heartstrings like never before...

Turn the page and let's begin

CHRISTMAS CHILD

"Good morning, Colonel, and you, too, Madam. May I wish you both a very merry Christmas." The butler entered the breakfast room with a covered platter of hot sausages, bacon, eggs, smoked fish, and toast to serve the colonel and his lady personally, which he always did on special occasions.

"And we wish you the same, Perkins," replied his mistress. Her husband took the cover off the platter, and the delicious aroma of Christmas breakfast filled the room.

"There was a snowfall during the night," Mrs. Leigh-Donner said.

"It has begun again, Madam." Perkins looked toward the window, and their eyes followed his, just in time to see a carriage halt outside amid the whirling snowflakes.

"There is somebody out today," the colonel said. "It's too early to be Charlotte and the children. The neighbours have visitors, I expect."

The doorbell rang, startling them. Who could be at their door on Christmas morning?

"Excuse me," Perkins said, setting the platter down and making for the door.

"Very odd," remarked Colonel Leigh-Donner.

They heard voices in animated debate in the hallway.

Perkins burst into the room, rather quickly for his usual gravitas.

"It is a policeman, Colonel, to see you and Mrs. Leigh-Donner, and he bears a -" he stopped, for the constable was upon his heels and had entered the room. In his arms was a small child covered in a blanket, a woolly cap about the head. The child was asleep.

There was amazement.

"What, is he injured? Lay him on the easy chair, and we will fetch a doctor." Mrs. Leigh-Donner assumed that there had been an accident outside their door.

"No, it is not that." Perkins was red-faced and very agitated. "The constable says there is a note come with her."

Trembling, he thrust a piece of paper into the colonel's hands. There, he read, in bold capital letters, the following words.

MY NAME IS EMMA. I WAS BORN ON 1ST JULY 1859 IN A COUNTRY FAR AWAY. PLEASE TAKE ME TO MY PATERNAL GRANDPARENTS AT 11 ELIZABETH STREET, BELGRAVIA.

"Emma! My own name!" Mrs. Leigh-Donner fainted.

"She was found last night at Victoria Station in the ladies waiting room," said the constable. "She spent the night at the police station, wrapped up as warm as they could make 'er. Where shall I set the child?" He was getting impatient, for he wished to be rid of his burden, and he was forming the idea that the couple at this address had no wish to be acquainted with the child. It was a long way to a workhouse, and he had no wish to go there in a snowfall.

The housekeeper, Mrs. Breen, appeared then, and having been shown the note by Mr. Perkins, took the child from the constable, who made a hurried departure.

Assistance was found for her mistress, who was recovering. The colonel was stricken dumb.

"I shall take the child downstairs and give her milk," said Mrs. Breen. "What a shock!"

THE SONS

Mrs. Leigh-Donner was able to sip some hot coffee and managed a slice of toast and a little poached egg. The colonel ate a hearty breakfast. He always said that eating helped him to think, and not even a shock like this would cause him to neglect his Christmas breakfast.

"Grandparents indeed! She cannot be our family," Emma said flatly. "Our boys are good boys."

The colonel said nothing. He had been in the army a long time and knew that plenty of young men sowed their wild oats while their mothers at home thought them saints.

They had two living sons, and neither was in England. Wesley was in India, a bachelor, he planned to marry when he returned on his next leave. He would hardly risk his chances with Lady Margaret Winston by sending home evidence of an indiscretion.

Lewis was in Italy on a European tour. They were in regular contact with Lewis; he was destined for Oxford and the Church. It could not be Lewis.

A silence ensued as there was one name left.

"Could it be…could it possibly be Cyril?" Emma asked in a very, very quiet voice.

The breakfast room was hung with doubt and possibility, hope and despair.

"No, it cannot be Cyril," her husband replied flatly and somewhat derisively.

"But, suppose he is alive?"

Cyril, the oldest son, was a captain in the British Army and had been missing, presumed dead, in the Crimea five years before.

"How could he be alive and not come home? How could he be alive and father a child in adultery? Have sense, Emma. Eat something."

"Charlotte will not like it," she admitted then, "if he is alive, and did not come home to her, and neglected her and the children all this time, and perhaps stayed in the Crimea and had a second family."

"It is a preposterous thought! Put it out of your head!"

"But he may be alive, just think! What if my Cyril is alive all this time! They never confirmed he was dead. They never found the bodies."

"He is dead, as are Corporals Brown and Enright."

Captain Cyril Leigh-Donner had led Corporals Richard Brown and James Enright up a steep hill on a scouting mission. An hour after they had left, the camp had heard shots from the hill. They had never been seen or heard of again in spite of extensive searches. They knew all three. Brown had been a young footman and Enright the coachman in the Leigh-Donner household. It had been a dreadful blow when they had heard the devastating news. The house had gone into a long mourning. The parents of the other two men lived in Spitalfields and Whitechapel, only a few miles from each other. Mrs. Leigh-Donner had visited them and given them consolation and help.

Mrs. Leigh-Donner rang the bell and ordered the child to be brought up to them. When she arrived, she was taken in her arms while she scrutinised her keenly.

"If you're looking for a resemblance, all infants look the same," her husband said, annoyed.

"She is getting past the infant stage, when resemblances begin to form. Do you not think that her eyes could look like ours, a little?"

"It's your imagination, Emma. Do not even begin to dream that Cyril is alive. This is not Cyril's child. He did not have fair hair."

She rumpled the thick fair tresses.

"Hair colour often changes!"

The child was awake and Emma, feeling restless, walked with her about the room. They came to a cabinet upon which was a group of photographs.

"Papa," sang the little one, pointing straight at a head and shoulders photo of Cyril.

"She is Cyril's! She is!" Mrs. Leigh-Donner became very excited. The colonel sighed in frustration and gulped back his coffee. If his son was alive and well somewhere, and in his wits, he was not only an adulterer, but a deserter and a disgrace. Better to believe him dead!

"It's Christmas morning, and Charlotte and the children will be here soon. Is all well with the kitchen preparations? Get your wits about you, Mrs. Leigh-Donner!" His black bushy eyebrows, the terror of his men, were drawn together in a frown.

"Yes, of course."

"Send the child down to the servants and we shall see what is to be done with her later on."

Mrs. Leigh-Donner pulled the bell again.

"Is my Cyril alive?" she asked herself, caressing her son's photograph. There must be some strange explanation for this, an explanation in which her son would come out blameless of course. He had lost his memory. That was it!

He had married and regained his memory. But her ideas petered out in the improbability of it all.

CHARLOTTE'S ALARM

The housekeeper and butler said nothing downstairs about the note, and the staff were astounded at the sudden appearance of a child in their midst. She was placed in the care of the under housemaid while the servants prepared for their guests, Mrs. Cyril Leigh-Donner and her three children and their nursemaid.

They arrived at two o'clock full of Christmas merriment and gifts for their grandparents and sat down to a table laden with roast turkey stuffed with pork, baked ham dripping with syrup, golden roast potatoes, brussels sprouts, carrots, and lashings of gravy, with wine for the adults and lemonade for the children. But Charlotte noticed something wrong. Her parents-in-law were always a little sad about Cyril at Christmas, but always made the effort for the sake of the children. Today, even the jovial Grandfather was drawn and silent.

After sending the children out to play in the back garden after the Christmas pudding had been served, she asked them what the matter was. They had no choice but to inform her of the morning's happenings and to show her the note.

"It can't be Cyril," she said, her voice tremulous.

"Why not?" her mother-in-law asked sharply.

"He is dead."

"Quite so, Charlotte," Colonel Leigh-Donner said.

Charlotte's hands were shaking; she put her coffee cup back on the saucer with a giveaway tinkle. She had fallen out of love with Cyril a few years after they married, and he with her. They had been very young, she seventeen, he twenty. He had not been a bad man, but authoritarian like his father, and she had begun to suffer under his tight control and domineering way. While she never wished him dead, after seven years she would be free to remarry if he did not return. She was in love again, and Mr. Marshall was patiently waiting until she could be declared free.

"It cannot be Cyril," she said flatly.

"She pointed to his portrait and said 'Papa,'" Mrs. Leigh-Donner said firmly. There was a very uncomfortable silence.

"What will you do with her?" Charlotte asked.

"We do not know," her father-in-law said.

"It must be a hoax," Charlotte went on. "It is well known you have a son missing, presumed dead, and someone wants a good place for their illegitimate, nobody child. Is there no way to find out for certain?"

"It appears there is not," Mrs. Leigh-Donner said. "Her clothes are not of the best quality but decent, and she is clean. She has been taken care of. She has a few words, but they are unintelligible."

After dinner, Charlotte went downstairs to the servant's hall to see the child for herself. She was sleeping on a small couch, two chairs drawn up close to it to prevent her from falling off. She gazed at her and satisfied herself that she looked nothing like Cyril's other children.

"She looks common," was her verdict. "It's a hoax, a deception, to get her a good life. She has a cunning parent who would risk that, but it is so cruel to pretend that Cyril is alive, when he is not! And why do my in-laws not think of their other two sons? It would be a good trick indeed, for either of them, to point a finger at Cyril's being alive, when they know he is not."

When her mother-in-law asked her to take the baby home with her because she had a nursery, she refused, and left that evening in a very bad temper. Unlike the first Christmas, this Christmas had been ruined by the arrival of a small child.

A HOME IS FOUND

It was only a matter of time before the servants at 11 Elizabeth Street knew the entire story of the new arrival. A word overheard here and there, and they knew that the child was thought to be a grandchild of the old couple, and there were some hot debates as to which of the sons could be responsible. Some held out for Master Wesley, for he was a wild one, always had been, always in some scrape or other. Who knew what he was up to out there in India? Some thought that if it were Master Lewis, he could not now become a clergyman.

But what of Master Cyril? News of his possible survival travelled quickly to the Enright and Brown families, and they soon turned up to take a view of the child, finding any possible resemblance that would show their son and brother alive.

"She's Jim's, I know it, that little face she made there, when she looked around, that was 'is."

"She 'as my son's eyes, and my daughter's small 'ands."

"No, fer she's too tall fer your son. Your son was well built, but he couldn't ever be said to be tall."

"Your Jim was forever making faces orright. But I can't see anyfink of 'im in that little one."

They wanted to claim her, and yet they did not want to claim her, for the same reason as the colonel had. Their sons had died bravely in the service of Queen and Country and were no deserters. But the possibility that she was their flesh and blood was dangled in front of them. To add to the complicated situation, Emma called every man in a handlebar moustache 'Papa.' Mrs. Leigh-Donner was disappointed to hear this and witness it for herself, for Emma had pointed to two tradesmen and the next-door footman who sported the moustaches and said the magic word.

Charlotte was desperate to pin little Emma down on one of the above families, to get her moved away from Belgravia, out of her sight and out of her in-laws' lives. But which family was most likely to take her? The Browns were very poor and shabby. Mrs. Brown had stated that her son had been born to her late in life, and perhaps it would not be fair upon them or upon the child to make parents of them at this stage of their lives, even if they were willing.

The Enrights were younger, neat of dress, and had a sensible look about them, and their home address was better than that of the Spitalfields family. She took the carriage to Lilac Lane, Whitechapel, and called upon Mrs. Enright in her modest two-up-two-down home, who said that she doubted very much that the child was Jim's.

"I am willing to pay you fifty pounds a year for her keep if you take her," she declared, panic-stricken.

Fifty pounds a year was not to be sniffed at.

"I will take her then," Mrs. Enright said, with great dignity.

The Browns were furious with the Enrights. When they heard about the money, they were sure that Emma was a Brown. But Mrs. Enright would not listen and outfitted her house as best she could for a small child, getting a little cot for her to sleep in, good second-hand frocks and pinnies, and putting everything up high. The money enabled her to employ a maid to do all the extra work that having a small child in the house would create.

Mr. Enright was adamant about one aspect of taking the toddler in.

"She can't 'ave our name, Berry, fer that means our son is alive and a deserter."

"What name shall we give 'er then?" Mrs. Enright had not thought about this, but she would not have Jim's name besmirched among their neighbours in Lilac Lane. There must be no doubt about their Jim's heroism.

"Her proper name of course, that of Leigh-Donner."

"No, Jack. That's a 'andful. Make it either Leigh or Donner."

They flipped a coin, heads Leigh, tails Donner, and it came out heads. They then put it about that the colonel could not bear the disgrace of their son being a deserter and had fostered her out to cover up the scandal. They were very confident that he would never find out that they had used the Leigh name, but not knowing how to spell it, they used 'Lee.'

THE MOORES

Indignant correspondence from the two junior Leigh-Donners denying paternity of the little girl reassured their parents that they had taken the correct course in letting Emma go. She was no responsibility of theirs. They soon forgot that disturbing Christmas morning and settled themselves back into the view they had had before, that Cyril was dead. They were fond of Charlotte, and they were happy to welcome Mr. Marshall into their family as her new husband. She would have somebody to look after her, and the children had a new father. Mrs. Leigh-Donner got over her disappointment and wondered how she could ever have thought that Cyril was alive, perhaps a deserter, and had behaved so ill toward his wife.

Little Emma was raised at 4 Lilac Lane, Whitechapel. It was a rough place, and not far away were the large tenement buildings that housed hundreds of families.

Many of the children she knew came from there, but her favourite friend was a boy named Patrick Moore, who lived in No. 5 across the road, in a house similar to hers.

Patrick was one of a large family. His father worked in the Hodges Type Foundry and was a sober family man. His mother saw to it that the children never came out of the house with dirty faces or runny noses. All of the children had their tasks to do, the older helped with the younger, and they all knew how to darn and sew. Emma loved them. She loved nothing better than to go over to their house and play with the young Moores, and as often as not she took part in their little chores with them, for the younger children could fetch and carry.

Emma was lonely in her own house. She called the old couple Aunt and Uncle. They were old and sat in the parlour while she was sent to the kitchen to be with Sarah, the maid. Sarah was unkind. She splashed her with hot water and tried to trip her up with a broom. Sometimes Emma would cry, and her aunt would come and ask what the ruckus was. Emma would tell her, and Sarah would receive a mild reprimand, and that was all. She was free again to carry out her petty cruelties against the young child.

"Little Emma is come again," Mrs. Moore often observed to her husband when Emma opened the back door and came in. Sometimes she just stood inside the door, as if waiting, but saying nothing. Perhaps she was not sure of her welcome. Mrs. Moore would sigh and say, "Come on in then, Emma, the girls are playing upstairs." And the little child's face would light up, she would run through the kitchen, and they would hear her little feet clambering up to see her friends.

"It's not much of a life for 'er over there with those two old people," Mr. Moore would say.

"And that girl Sarah. She's 'orrid to her. She keeps the 'ouse clean and is a good cook and her laundry is spic and span, and they put up with the way she treats Emma."

"Will they send her to school, do you think?"

Children did not have to attend school, though there was a growing belief among all sections of society that all children, even girls, should be able to read and write. The Moores wanted this for their brood, and they were prepared to make sacrifices to pay for it. Mr. Moore had long ago switched to a cheaper brand of tobacco than that which he liked best, and he never took a cab. Mrs. Moore sat up late at night sewing clothes and walked two miles for her fish and eels because it was cheaper. They sacrificed for their children, whose names were Helen, Angela, Dennis, Mary, Patrick, and Lucy and Oliver who were twins. It was not a tidy house, as the Enrights' was, and it was all noise and clatter, making and mending, and there was a great deal of economy, but enough food and coal, and plenty of love. Mrs. Moore was perpetually tired, but she had learned that a tidy house was not worth the constant shouting, so she chose her battles. She wanted her children to grow up with faith in God and kindness to others, and they knew better than to cross her in these two matters. Once a year, one of her sisters came to look after the family for a week while she and Mr. Moore went to his brother in Brighton for a little holiday.

Patrick was a quiet, unassuming boy, but very intelligent. He saw things. He saw how the little girl from across the road, about three years younger than he, was lonely and sad. So he went out of his way to play with her and cheer her up, and she rewarded him with happy, dimpled smiles.

"Why did Emma come to live with 'er uncle and aunt?" he asked his father one day.

"Her mother and father are dead, I suppose," his father replied, but there was a vagueness to his reply, and Patrick knew that his father knew more than he was telling.

"She's Emma Lee, and her uncle and aunt are Enright."

"That don't signify. You're a Moore, aren't you? And you have an uncle and aunt named Smith."

This satisfied him for a time, but as Patrick grew, he knew better. Emma was not related to the Enrights, but to a rich family named Lee who lived in a posh part of the City, who paid the Enrights to look after her. The Lees never visited her, and she never visited them. He felt sorry for her, but did not mention anything to her about it, as she mightn't know and might feel hurt.

Emma was not to go to school, and Patrick was aghast. He was vexed with Emma's real family, the Lees, for not seeing to her schooling, and if he knew where they lived, he might get up the courage to go and complain. But he didn't know where they lived, and he was relieved that he did not have to get up his courage.

After complaining to his father, Mr. Moore paid a call to the Enrights. Why did the Lees not send the child to school? The Enrights took the hint. Emma found herself in the same school as the Moore children and was very happy there, for she was away from Sarah most of the time.

When she was with Sarah in the afternoons, she took out her copybook and pencil at the kitchen table and began to do her exercises. Sarah was quiet and left her alone. Unknown to Emma, she was jealous. She had never been to school and could not read. Emma now had an advantage over her, and she felt her own inferiority. She did not speak to her or disturb her. Emma had no idea why Sarah had stopped tormenting her, but she thought it was because Mr. Moore had said something to her also. In her eyes, Mr. Moore was a powerful man. She sometimes pretended that he was her father, and that Mrs. Moore was her mother.

Sometimes, the children at school said strange things to her, like her father was a rich man, or her father was a coward, which made her cry. One day she questioned her aunt about where she had come from, and Aunt Berry told her she had been delivered to them one Christmas morning, wrapped up in a blanket with a big red bow. A few of the girls in her class had no parents either and lived with relatives. Her aunt and uncle bought her nice toys at Christmas and on her birthday and did not beat her, but she wished they were young and would take her to the park or to the fair. However, the Moores had few new toys and she always shared hers with them when she went across the street. She was generous in sharing with them. But she could not ask them to come to her house. Her uncle and aunt did not want them there because they made too much noise.

Many of the families around them had new babies every year or so, including Mrs. Moore. None of them arrived on the doorsteps with a big bow, and Emma was mystified as to why she had been the only one that had come like that, until she was old enough to understand. Mary Moore whispered the truth to her one day in great excitement. The baby grew in Mama's tummy.

"But I was put on the doorstep," Emma objected.

"Then you was born somewhere else," Mary said knowingly.

BABY WILLIAM

When Patrick was fourteen, he was taken out of school to join his father in the Foundry. He did not like leaving school but accepted that his wages were needed now to help the family. His older brother and sisters were all working, and two older sisters were about to be married.

Emma went to the Moore house one day to find that all of the children were gone to stay with their Grandmother Smith, and Mrs. Enright said that it was because a new baby was coming to the house. She kept a close eye on the Moore doorstep, but nothing arrived. Yet Mrs. Enright announced that there was a new baby boy across the street.

"This'll be Mrs. Moore's last," she heard her whisper to Mrs. Lowe, a visiting neighbour. "She told me she was forty-two, and thought she was finished, and then she found out she was in the puddin' club again."

None of this made any sense to Emma, and she knew that she had to wait patiently for a few days to see the new child.

He was a beautiful boy named William, and she loved him right away. He became her favourite Moore after Patrick, and his mother was pleased, for she helped. She rocked the cradle to get him to sleep, and she held him when he cried until his mother was ready to take and feed him.

"You're nearly part of the family, aren't you?" Mrs. Moore said to her, and her heart soared. Would she be able to come and live here, and be a proper part of the family?

"Maybe I'll change my name to Emma Moore," she said brightly.

"Who knows, indeed." Mrs. Moore smiled mysteriously. "Now can you be a good girl and get me a fresh towel from the cupboard? I declare I don't know where Mary and Lucy have got to today. Mary! Come and get the table ready! The men will be 'ome soon!"

Patrick was considered a man now, as he was earning, as was his older brother Dennis, who was eighteen.

Emma held the baby while Mary flew around the kitchen getting supper ready. She looked down at the pink baby skin, soft dark hair, and chubby little fingers. The baby made her feel tender, sweet, and loving.

I want a baby someday, she thought. A baby just like William. I will get married and have lots of children!

MONEY DRIES UP

While Emma was dreaming of getting married someday and filling her home with children, she had no idea that her future could be gravely affected by a conversation taking place in a wealthy part of London.

"It's gone on long enough," Mr. Marshall told his lady. "Fifty pounds a year to support a child who isn't even a Leigh-Donner! Fifty pounds! We have six children now, Charlotte."

"I know, but how do I stop it? The Enrights expect it now."

"It should never have begun," Mr. Marshall said.

"I told you before many times," Charlotte said patiently, "that I wanted that child gone from our lives. Mrs. Enright would not have taken her without the fifty pounds a year. Nobody knows who the child really is, and she had to disappear. I could not send her to the workhouse. I'm not heartless."

"Yes, my dear, but there was no onus on you to provide for her. That could be interpreted as an admission of responsibility."

"It was a charity, no more." Charlotte said unhappily.

"You must have been truly afraid that she was Cyril's child," her husband replied.

Every year, there was a quarrel about the money to be paid to the Enrights when it was time to take fifty pounds from the bank, place it in an envelope, and give it to the coachman to deliver to the address in Whitechapel, usually on the first Sunday in January.

"Our own children need this money," George said, "not this waif from nowhere. We shall not pay it anymore. Fifty pounds! Ten would have been ample!"

Charlotte was silent. What her husband had said was true. The payments would have to cease. She had already laid out a very great sum, just to keep the Enrights happy to keep her.

"I have been foolish in this matter, George. No doubt that by now they are very fond of her, and would not even notice that we have ceased the payments."

She hoped that was true. Christmas came and went, and New Years Day fell on a Sunday.

MILK AND CAKE!

"It's the first Sunday in January, and it oughter come today," Mrs. Enright said to her husband.

"I wouldn't bank on it," he replied. "For it being an 'oliday. I would wait until tomorrow. It'll come tomorrow."

But the coach did not come on the morrow. Nor the day after.

"They wrote off New Years Day as the first Sunday, and have fixed next Sunday as the proper day," Mr. Enright said.

Emma knew that every year, a man came to the door with an envelope for her uncle and aunt. He never stayed longer than to hand it over and then vanished. She did not know what the envelope contained, but it was thick, and she never saw it again. She concluded that there must be money in it, for a shopping spree always followed, and she got new clothes made, always too big for her but she grew into them.

The second Sunday in January came and went, and no man appeared with the envelope. Emma knew her uncle and aunt were restless and fidgety as darkness set in.

"You'd better go and see about it," Mrs. Enright ordered.

"I don't even know where the lady lives!"

"You know where the main family live and you can find out where the other is! Emma, go upstairs. Mr. Enright and I are talking."

She trudged up the stairs to her little room, rather alarmed. Something was wrong. Her uncle and aunt were on tenterhooks for the week, worried about something. There was a disagreement.

Mr. Enright insisted on letting a third Sunday pass. That was enough; Mrs. Enright would have no more delay.

"Take 'er wiv you to frighten 'em," his wife commanded.

"How could that be fair?"

"Take 'er! Maybe they 'eard she was dead or somefink!"

And so it came to pass that Emma set out with her uncle on a mysterious trip across London on the top of an omnibus. She was delighted, for she was never taken anywhere. She drank in all the sights and sounds of the busy streets, so much grander than Whitechapel! After they disembarked the bus, her uncle led her down a quiet street with tall, gracious buildings like a row of fine ladies dressed in white.

"Where are we, Uncle?"

"This is Elizabeth Street."

"Why is it called that?"

"To honour Good Queen Bess, I suppose."

"Are the people very rich here? I mean, does only one family live in one big 'ouse?"

"Yes, of course they do. They're gentry. Toffs. Look 'igh up there, see the attic windows. The servants sleep up there. They work in the basements. Come and look over these railings. There's a big kitchen down there. The family, the rich people, eat meat at every sitting-down, and butter and cream. Then there's a back stairs up to the attics. My sister was a servant hereabouts once. Very cold attics."

"I'm glad I'm not a servant, then," Emma said. "Why are we 'ere, Uncle?"

"We have business," he said and knocked on a dark blue door. The number 11 was on a shiny plaque on the door.

What happened next was very puzzling to Emma. The snooty man who opened it was rude. Her uncle was asking to speak to 'the guvnor' who she knew was an important man. But 'the guvnor' was not in. The 'guvnor's wife' was not in either, and the door was slammed.

Undaunted, Uncle Enright said to her "wait 'ere," and he took the stairs down to the basement where the staff worked. He came up again with a smile upon his face. "They remember my Jim, and the cook told me where I should go. Come on, we 'ave another journey to do now." So they walked several streets again and he knocked upon another door, this time a red one. This time, he asked for 'Mrs. Marshall' and was admitted.

Emma found herself in a large and beautiful room. She could not take her eyes off the blue velvet chairs and curtains. A soft carpet was underfoot; she had never walked upon the like. Paintings in gold frames hung everywhere, and the wallpaper was of silver and white stripes. There was a glass creation hanging down from the ceiling, sparkling in the light.

She reached out and touched the back of a chair, withdrawing her hand quickly when the door opened.

A woman entered the room, her eyebrows raised, a flush coming over her cheeks when she saw her guests.

"What is this about?"

"I fear, Mrs. Marshall, there 'as been some misunderstanding."

"Who are you?" Mrs. Marshall knew very well who he was.

"You must remember, Mrs. Marshall. I'm Jack Enright, and we had an agreement many years ago, regarding –"

Suddenly Emma became aware that she was the object of attention. She looked from her uncle to the woman, puzzled. She squirmed and felt uncomfortable.

Mrs. Marshall was not a woman without feeling; she was a mother, and she went to the window and pulled the bell.

"Let us say no more for the present, Mr. Enright. Be seated please." They waited. Emma sat gingerly upon one of the plush chairs. No more was said until a maid in a black dress, a white apron, and elaborate white cap entered.

"Elsie, take this girl to the kitchen and give her milk and cake."

"Yes, ma'am." Elsie looked surprised but motioned Emma to follow her. When they had left the room, Mrs. Marshall turned on the old man and spoke with reproach.

"How could you, Mr. Enright? Bring the girl here? And talk of our arrangement in front of her? Have you no feeling?"

"I thought you might like proof she was alive, Madam. We 'ad an arrangement, and this year, there has been some delay. If it is to be forthcoming, forgive my coming 'ere. But I thought I should come to report we received noffink, in case you 'ad sent your representative with it and there had been some mis'ap. We never received our fifty pounds."

"There will be no more money, Mr. Enright. We have been generous."

"Excuse me, Madam. We had an arrangement. No more money indeed! We can't afford to keep 'er!"

"She may well be your blood, Mr. Enright!"

"And she may be yours, Madam!"

"Or neither of ours!"

"Well tha's it, isn't it, Madam? Nobody knows. But your first 'usband's family 'ave the most claim, taking the name of Emma, and being left specifically for your in-laws. You got rid of 'er, for it would complicate matters."

"She does not resemble us in the least, Mr. Enright."

Mrs. Marshall stood up, indicating the interview to be over.

"I consider we have done even more than obliged to, if obligation there ever was, for the girl. Surely you have grown fond of her?" Her voice was a little desperate, for being a mother, concern for the innocent child intruded.

"Of course we're fond of 'er. We luv 'er! But she's not ours, she don't resemble our Jim in the least. Or any of the cousins. None of 'em."

"That doesn't signify. My children do not resemble their cousins at all. Now I must ask you to leave." She pulled the bell again. "See the girl up to the street," she instructed Elsie this time. "Mr. Enright is leaving us."

When Emma was reunited with her uncle by the outside railings, his bad mood registered immediately.

"I kept you some cake, Uncle," she said, taking the crumbly object from her pocket.

"Eat it yourself. I'll 'ave nothing of theirs," he retorted with anger, though he was hungry.

"What was it about?"

"Noffink. Don't ask me anymore questions." She kept silent all the way home. She thought of the big kitchen, the large glass of creamy milk, the two slices of chocolate cake set in front of her by Elsie. There had been an old woman there who had looked at her with some curiosity, and a kitchen maid peeling vegetables. She had felt strange, but the milk was delicious, and she had never before tasted a cake that had chocolate in it. She kept thinking about it all that evening.

WHAT WILL BECOME OF HER

The atmosphere in the Enright family was tense, and Emma knew that she was somehow involved but did not know how. She tried to catch snatches of conversation between her uncle and aunt. Her aunt was a little deaf and so her uncle had to raise his voice sometimes.

"Try the Browns! You're the proper person to go there, for you and Mrs. Brown were friends!"

Her aunt said something she couldn't make out.

"I never 'eard 'e was dead..."

The door slammed shut and Emma knew she was not meant to hear whatever else was being said.

The non-arrival of the fancy coach and the mysterious visitor to the Enrights had not gone unnoticed in the neighbourhood. The Enrights weren't getting any more money from the toffs who had fostered out the girl to them. Everybody knew that the girl delivered to Elizabeth Street on Christmas morning was the daughter of a captain in the Army. He was a deserter and a bigamist, and to protect the family's reputation, Emma had been fostered out.

"So what will 'appen to her now?" Mrs. Moore whispered to Mrs. Cadwell, a friend who had a large family also, and was visiting to return the soft newborn gowns she'd borrowed for her baby. Mrs. Moore made a cup of tea and they sat at the table, the tea well out of reach of their youngest children who sat upon their laps. They had mastered the art of speaking in whispers, for little pitchers have big ears, and they would have been dismayed to learn that too much of what they said to each other was overheard by those little pitchers anyway.

"The colonel's family are not going to pay 'em anymore, Maisie. Jack and Berry are annoyed as can be. And they're right too."

"What will happen to Emma now?"

"They won't keep 'er. They're going to take her down to old Mrs. Brown, to see if she'll do a turn. But Mrs. Brown was black as thunder when she heard that the Enrights had landed themselves fifty pounds a year to take her. She wouldn't speak to 'em after for years, in spite of their sons 'aving perished together on that hill. Here are the gowns

Maisie, washed an' all. I am very grateful for the use of 'em."

"I won't be needin' 'em again," Mrs. Moore whispered with a giggle. "Give them to Edie Jacobs, poor soul. She 'asn't two pennies to rub together, the way 'er man is, in the pub every night."

Patrick was no longer 'a little pitcher' and they took no notice of his presence in the scullery just off the kitchen. He was so quiet that sometimes people did not notice he was around. He was polishing all the boots in the family for Sunday Mass tomorrow.

He heard every word. His gentle heart went out to Emma.

YOU 'AVE 'IS MINCERS!

"Put on your cloak, Emma. You and I are payin' a visit to an old friend," Mrs. Enright ordered the young girl.

Emma was intrigued; a mysterious visit last week and now this. What was afoot? Were they going into the posh part of London again? Would there be another glass of creamy milk and chocolate cake?

But no. They walked and walked until they came to a crooked little street, with eight low houses crammed all together, as if giant hands had pressed them at each end. Mrs. Enright stopped at one in the middle, arguably the worst, with slats missing and broken windows stuffed with rags. Emma looked at it in distaste. Lilac Lane was dirty a lot of the time, but most residents there had pride and kept their houses as nice as they could.

A quavering voice bade them to come in, and they entered a dark, smoky room with a small coal fire burning at one end. Crouched almost on top of it, seated upon a stool, was an old woman in a tattered grey shawl. She was poking the fire.

"Shut the door quick!" she ordered, barking over her shoulder. "Who 'ave I 'ere?"

"It's Berry Enright, Harriet dear! It's been a long time since we met."

The old woman's face was lit by the firelight, and Emma saw a face of wrinkles and creases like crumpled paper, with two sharp eyes, a long nose, and a mouth without teeth. She smelled of the fire, and she smelled of fish.

"You! Arter all these years!"

"Yes, it's me, Berry Enright."

"And who's she?" A bony hand pointed to Emma.

"She's Emma. Do you remember Emma, Harriet?" Mrs. Enright pushed her forward.

The creases on the old woman's face seemed to flatten a little.

"Emma! I remember Emma! Richard's girl! Richard's girl, but you took the mint! Get out of 'ere, I want nuffink to do wiv you. You can stay," she said to Emma. "I'll share anyfink I 'ave, what little I 'ave, wiv you. Come 'ere!" She grabbed her wrist, pulling her toward her with surprising strength. Emma drew back, her heart hammering with fright. Who was this mad old woman?

"Don't be afeard of me, Emma. You 'ave 'is mincers, luvly blue like the cornflowers! Small 'and, too, I see, like me ma. Come closer to the fire so I can get a proper butchers." She pulled her toward the firelight and put her face close to hers to get a better look, and Emma smelled her rotten teeth.

She screamed, broke free, ran from the house, and stood outside it, sobbing with fright and trembling all over. She was joined by her aunt a moment later.

"There, Emma, there's noffink to be frightened of, don't take on so." Mrs. Enright put an arm about the girl's shoulders.

"Aunt Berry, what's she talking about?"

"Don't mind 'er, she's mad as an 'atter. I paid a call to find out as 'ow she was. We 'ad a difference some years ago."

"Whose eyes was she talking about, Aunt? Who's Richard?"

"Her son who was killed in the war out foreign. He was with my son. Everyone she meets she says is like 'im. Don't worry 'bout it. Near everybody in England 'as blue mincers. Take no notice."

But Emma did worry. There was something bad afoot, and it all had to do with her. *You took the mint.* Was that the envelope that arrived every New Years except this one?

"I won't 'ave to go and stay with 'er, will I? Say I won't, Aunt Berry! I don't want to go there ever again!"

"Tha's orright, pet, you won't ever 'ave to see that old bat again, I promise you."

She did not hear the conversation between the adults that night when Mrs. Enright recounted the visit to her husband, for they had been careful to shut the door.

"Emma was terrified; she ran out of the 'ouse screamin' blue murder. I was frightened enough myself. That old woman is batty. She said Emma was like Dick about the eyes. Who knows? Maybe she's Dick's child. I wouldn't put it past 'im, fer 'e was always a rogue. But as for getting Mrs. Brown to take 'er, no, I'm not a beast, even if it was proved beyond doubt that she was a Brown. That woman ain't fit company for nobody outside a lunatic asylum. We'll keep 'er, Jack, but we'll 'ave to let Sarah go. Emma will 'ave to come out of school and do the 'ousework. She's a good girl, and do you know, Jack, I'm quite fond of 'er, though she's noffink to us in blood. Poor girl, if you could just 'ave seen how frighted she was today, with that old hag clawing at 'er wrist, my 'eart went out to her and I realised 'ow much I like her, poor pet. She'll be truly ours from now on, and let those toffs in Belgravia rot, and Harriet Brown is fer the asylum afore long."

Emma was disappointed to leave school. Now she had to stay at home and do all the housework, cooking, and washing. But as the year wore on, she settled a little better into her role and felt happier with herself. The unpleasant events of January faded, and her fears ceased. The Enrights were more caring and took a greater interest in what she was doing. They grew closer, and she was quite fonder of them as their dependence upon her grew. She understood how they liked things and strove to please them. The Moores were just across the street, and Mrs. Enright now welcomed the girls over to visit, because they were not noisy anymore. She sometimes gave Emma some money to spend on herself, for she was growing up, and young girls need ribbons and little bits of finery.

The years passed quickly.

Patrick was also a frequent visitor, and sometimes he took his sisters and Emma out to the park or to a fair, and they once went to a music hall. He knew he was in love with Emma, and he had no eyes for anybody else. She had grown beautiful with thick wavy fair hair and large almond shaped blue eyes, the bluest he had ever seen, and soft creamy skin. Her warm, dimpled smile captured his heart. He ventured to hold her hand, and she did not object, as Mary and Lucy hung behind wherever they went, to allow them to converse together.

The Moore parents watched the relationship grow with affection. "She said she would one day become Emma Moore," said the mother, "and though she did not mean it as in becoming a wife, I think she'll be our daughter-in-law one day."

But cruel fate overtook the happy times. Mr. Enright became ill and died within a short time. Mrs. Enright suffered a severe stroke. Emma nursed her at home. The old lady had lost the power of speech, and Emma knew she wished to say something, but could not. Her eyes were full of appeal, regret, and longing, all together. What was she trying to say? Was it related to the events of when she was eleven years old, events that stuck in Emma's mind and sometimes made her anxious? She knew that she had to leave school because the money had not been delivered, and that somehow the money was tied up with her. But it was frustrating not to know the entire story! Now, she would never know, and she would have to be content with not knowing. She could not bear the unhappiness in Mrs. Enright's eyes.

"It's all right," Emma said, patting her hand to relieve Mrs. Enright of her mental agony. "Everything is orright. I'll be fine."

The worried old brow cleared, her hand received a grateful squeeze, and Mrs. Enright slipped away that night, holding a framed photo of Jim that Emma had put into her hands.

THE GIFT

The afternoon of the funeral, Emma was in the house alone. Patrick had come to the funeral and gone straight back to work, and the neighbours had dispersed each to their own business after a cup of tea with her. The front door was unlocked, and Emma, who was washing the teacups, heard the noise of several people coming in. She dashed to the outer room to see Mrs. Enright's nephews, three men all much older than her, and two other men. The nephews had come to the graveyard and then quickly disappeared, and now here they were again, swarming through the little house, going into every room, issuing orders to the men.

"What are you doing?" Emma asked, alarmed.

"This house is goin' up for sale," Ben, the eldest, informed her. "We're takin' everything out of it."

"You can't!" Emma began to sob.

"We can. It's all mine," Ben said. "They made no will and I'm the closest kin. Go and pack up your own things, and I'll have a lock on this door tonight. And stop snivellin'. You 'ad a good run 'ere since the money stopped. Go back to yer own people."

They got to work and rushed past her as if she were not there. She saw a horse and cart out on the street, and without delay ran up to her little room to gather her belongings. The men were already there and had begun to strip it.

"Get out of my room!" she said with fury. "Give me at least a little privacy, you 'orrid set of thugs!" They were ashamed and left, and she banged the door and packed her bag.

They stripped the house of everything, every stick of furniture and every ornament, every cup and saucer, every lamp, every candle, even the half-burnt ones. They took all of Aunt's clothes and her jewellery, not that she had much, but she had a nice piece or two for special occasions. They rolled up the floor mats and the mattresses, threw the sheets and towels into boxes and piled everything upon the cart.

The neighbouring women gathered outside and shouted abuse at the men. "Yer aunt ain't cold in 'er grave!" "Buried this mornin' and look at you!" "I 'ope there's a downpour afore you reach 'ome!" but they took no notice.

Within two hours, the only home she could remember living in was bare of everything and locked up with a padlock. The cart, laden with dear and familiar items, disappeared around the corner. Mrs. Moore told Emma to come and stay in their house.

"If you 'ad't taken me in, Mrs. Moore, I would 'ave 'ad to sleep on the streets! All I 'ave is this little bag of clothes and a few shillin's."

"Don't worry, Emma luv. Everythin' will be orright in the end. God will look after you."

God! She knew nothing about God. The Enrights had not bothered much with going to church, and there had been no Bible or prayer book in their house. God was a remote Being, very far away. She did not want to be rude to Mrs. Moore, so she did not reply to her. What was she to do?

She thought that helping Mrs. Moore around the house would be enough to pay for her keep, but in this she was mistaken. She liked to see Patrick, his father, and his brother come home from the foundry and the cosy family evenings they had all together, though sometimes the young men went down to the pub, but they never came home the worse for "rink.

"I think, Emma, that you will 'ave to go away soon for work," Mr. Moore told her after four weeks, with a measured calm and kindness. "We can't afford to keep you 'ere, much as we would like to. Mrs. Moore 'as been making enquiries on your behalf. There is a vacancy at the house in Norland Square where our Angela was in service before she married. It's in Kensington, not too far away."

The housekeeper, who had loved Angela Moore, took 'Emma Lee' without even an interview, on the word of Mrs. Moore. They were expecting guests soon and she was hard put to find enough staff.

Patrick and the family made her going as easy as possible, and they told her that she was to consider their house her home, and to come on her days off to visit, but she felt rejected. Mary was working in a shop in Whitechapel, it was true. Lucy was to go to work as soon as she was old enough. So she reasoned with herself that they were not getting rid of her. It just felt as if they were.

The night before she left, Patrick took her for a walk. The house across the street now had a FOR SALE sign, and she hated to see it. It had been the only home she could remember in her life, and Lilac Lane the only neighbourhood she could remember living in. She missed the Enrights and was very uncertain as to her happiness in this large, mysterious house she was to enter the following morning. It loomed before her in her imagination like a large ghostly mansion with terrors around every corner and forbidding faces shrouded in elaborate white caps like Elsie the maid in the only posh house that she had ever been in.

"Cheer up, Emma. It will be orright. Angela liked it there well enough."

"I wish I knew what ter expect."

"I got you somethin'," Patrick said a little awkwardly, producing a little box from his pocket. They had taken a turn to walk under some trees that were swaying gently in the wind, and they halted underneath.

"What is it? For me?" Emma took it, and forgetting her anxiety for a moment, opened it with eagerness.

It was a pretty bracelet, not a cheap bangle, but something like Mrs. Enright would have brought out of her top drawer for special occasions like he' nieces' weddings. She slipped it upon her wrist.

"Ooh, it's beautiful, thank you," she said, tears falling from her eyes.

"Oh, never mind those tears now." Patrick leaned toward her and wiped her cheek with his thumb. She looked up at him, and then he asked her if he could kiss her. She nodded, and they shared a chaste kiss under the trees.

"Don't forget me, Emma.'

"I won't forget you, Pat."

They walked home and she admired her bracelet all the way there. She had never owned such a pretty thing before.

IN SERVICE

Emma worked hard in service at the house in Norland Square. It belonged to a judge who was a member of the House of Lords. She found him forbidding and avoided him as much as possible. His wife and daughters wore silks and satins, enormous hats, and elaborate jewellery. They were a very fashionable couple, and their house was elegant, with expensive furnishings and the best that money could buy. They entertained lavishly, and from time to time, the house was filled with other very fashionable people.

Her old uncle had been correct; servants' attics were cold. She had to share a bed with another maid, Sandra, and they arose to a frigid room with the water in the jug frozen. They rose every morning at five o'clock and prepared the house for the waking of the family, who expected to see warm fires and smell breakfast cooking, and everything about them sparkling and polished. The housekeeper, Mrs. Bowles, had a keen eye for dust and was constantly at war with it. She had taken a liking to Emma when she heard how she had cared for her aged uncle and aunt, and she felt motherly toward her, for Mrs. Moore had related her sorry tale, except for her real parentage. That would not do, for that might spell trouble down the road, and Mrs. Bowles might refuse to take her. Mrs. Moore had said she was an orphan.

Emma began to settle into the hard routine, but the food in the servant's hall was good, there was plenty of it, and she had a healthy appetite. After a year, her anxieties ceased, but a new thought or feeling began to enter her head.

As she took up and dusted the many valuable ornaments with care, the feelings grew until they began to occupy her even when she was not doing her work.

How nice it is for some people to have all these good things! I will never be able to afford gold candlesticks or sparkling crystal glasses. I will never be able to live in a house like this as one of the family, but only as a maid. The tablecloth in the dining room is the finest damask; I can only dream of a tablecloth like that. The bed sheets are pure linen, and when they're threadbare in the middle they give them to us, the servants! And get new ones for themselves! I only have one good hat, and Miss Carmichael has five, and she is no older than me! My best hat is worth far less than her worst hat! What I would not give to have a life like they have. And their jewellery! I have none. Nobody has ever given me anything, except that bracelet Patrick gave me. It cost him most of his wages, I think. How little Patrick earns!

She had loved her little bracelet, but when she saw the wealthy woman dripping with gold, silver, emeralds, and rubies, her bracelet lost much of its shine in her eyes, and so did Patrick and his limited wages in the foundry, where he worked so hard for so very little. He visited her every Sunday rain or shine, and if they had other time off that coincided, they always spent it together. He took her out, and she always had a good time. They talked about being engaged soon. She envisaged her future in a house like the one in Lilac Lane, though they would not be able to afford it for many years, and would have to live in a flat or half a house. The prospect did not enthrall her, and though she wanted to spend her life with Patrick Moore, she wondered how he could earn more money so that they could live well.

Envy began to worm its way into all of her thoughts, so that soon, Emma was becoming unhappy, very unhappy with her lot in life. She did not just want to not be a servant, she began to want to be rich. That seemed impossible, and she became angry and resentful in her heart, while outwardly courteous and suitably respectful to her employers and their guests, obeying every order with the attitude they expected. Were the other servants as unhappy and resentful as she? She could not see signs in them. Sandra was content enough, Edith, the senior parlourmaid, was even-tempered and hardworking and in her own practical way, ambitious.

"Do you not ever want to 'ave the nice things they 'ave?" Emma questioned them one evening as they sat around the kitchen table sewing or mending. "Those Wedgwoods, silver tea sets, and jewellery."

Edith broke off a thread with her teeth. "I'm going to be a housekeeper someday," she said.

"Don't you want to get married?" Sandra asked.

"No, not particularly. If I can keep myself, I'll be 'appy. If I'm a housekeeper, I'll 'ave my own little sitting room with china, rugs, and all I need, and will be very cosy. I put by for my old age, and I'll have enough to buy a beautiful cottage."

"I would like to marry," Sandra had said. "A handsome tradesman, sober. I'll 'ave my own house if he's 'ardworking, and I'm not going to marry a lazy fellow, so that excludes you, Frankie!"

The footman laughed at her. "I wouldn't put up wiv your naggin' at me for one second," he said.

"What of you, Emma? What do you want?" Edith asked her. Edith was about thirty, and the other servants regarded her as wise. "You said you like nice things. Will they make you 'appy, nice things? What's so good about havin' gold candlesticks and chandeliers?"

"I haven't really thought why it would be good," Emma admitted. "Except that I know I want 'em."

"If something goes missing, we know where to look then," Frankie chortled. "Under Emma's bed!"

"I'm not going to steal things."

"So how're you goin' to get 'em?" Sandra asked.

"She's going to marry a rich old fellow," Edith said, threading another needle. "And what of you, Frankie?"

"I'll become a butler, and 'ave my own pantry, and I'll learn all about wines, for that'll look very well on my references. *An expert on fine wine and spends a lot of time in the cellar.*"

They all laughed at this.

Emma felt that she did not fit in with the servants. They travelled in a different world and were content to strive for what was possible to them in that world. Edith, Sandra, and Frankie had their own dreams, different from hers. She did not belong here, and she had no dreams about bettering herself in the world of servitude she found herself in.

She remembered something the horrid Ben had said to her: *Go back to your own people.*

Who were they?

'HER OWN PEOPLE'

"You're not yourself. What's the matter, luv?" Patrick slipped his arm around her waist as they walked toward the park. There was a great advantage to living in a square; there was a fine park, and free to rich and poor alike. "You're down in the dumps lately. I'm worrit about you, I am."

"You're so lucky, Patrick. You know who you are and who your mother and father are. I don't. It bothers me to no end sometimes. I don't know where I come from! Benjamin, that man who came to take everything from the 'ouse, he said to me that I had a 'good run' and to go back to my own people. He said something about money, too. And at school, the other children used to shout things at me, about my father bein' rich and a bad soldier and such. Am I the daughter of a soldier? Shall we sit here, Pat? I'm tired, I am. I'm always tired."

"I'm concerned for your 'ealth, Emma. Did you tell Mrs. Bowles you're tired? Maybe she'll give you ligh'er duties."

"No, for if she did, the others will be jealous. Do you know what I think, Pat? All these thoughts and wonderin's, they make me tired. I can't sleep at night for it sometimes. I never thought that much about it before, I think, because I was busy with my uncle and aunt, but they weren't my uncle and aunt. I know that. Oh I am so muddled!"

Patrick held her close and said nothing. He was deep in thought. Should he tell her what he knew? His heart felt heavy with the burden.

"You're very quiet. You know somethin', Pat? Do you know somethin' about me that I don't know?"

He made no reply.

"You do, you do! You 'ave to tell me, Patrick. If we're going to be married, how can you keep a secret like that from me?"

She was right. She had every right to know, and they could not marry without him sharing with her what he knew.

"All I know is what I heard my mother and father say. That the Enrights, God rest their souls, fostered you because your own family couldn't keep you. You see, there would've been a scandal. What do you know of your father?"

. . .

"Nuffink."

"Three soldiers were killed in the Crimea, in a war. Or so they thought, but one of 'em is alive an' must've married and 'ad you. They never found any bodies. Then you were sent to the Lees."

"The Lees! Do you know the Lees?"

"No, not at all. Me know the Lees! There was a Captain Lee. He was from Belgravia, his father is a colonel and very important. When you were sent to the Lees some years after he was presumed dead, with a note saying that the colonel was your grandfather, it was a shock to them, because it meant that he must be alive, and I heard Mrs. Enright tell my mother that the captain was married with children 'ere in England. And your name, Emma, is the name of the old colonel's wife."

"My grandmother!"

"The family could not bear the disgrace, cos he was a married man with children like I said, and if he were alive, and hadn't gone back to his regiment, that would mean 'e 'ad deserted. The colonel likely couldn't bear the disgrace of that. And so they fostered you with the Enrights, the family whose son was killed along with the other fellow, Corporal Brown."

"Corporal Brown"

"Yes, Dick Brown."

"Richard Brown‟"

"Yes! Dick is short for Richard right enough! They told you about him?"

"I met his mother!" The memory made her shiver. "An old hag by the fire in a dark crook'd 'ouse! She frightened me‟"

"How?"

"She said I was like Richard. But she was mad as a hatter. Mrs. Enright said she was for the asylum. No, I'm not one of *them*." Her tone was filled with revulsion.

There was a little pause.

"So my relations live in Belgravia," she said. And her tone was now wondering and bright.

"They won't acknowledge you, Emmy," he said sadly, caressing her shoulder, pulling her closer to him. "It's their loss, innit? And our gain, my family, that is."

She could not but remember the visit to the two large houses in Belgravia.

"I remember where I was taken to when I was eleven years old," she said. "The name of the street was Elizabeth after Good Queen Bess, and the number of the house was eleven. I remember it cos I was eleven at the time! A blue door! I knew it was somethin' about me, though my uncle refused to tell me anything! And the blue door was shut in our faces and Uncle found out from the kitchen, I think, the name of another woman, Mrs. Marshall she was! She 'in't want to talk opposite me and sent me to the kitchen. And where is my father now? And my mother? Was I born in that other country, the Crimea? Where on earth is the Crimea? Am I even English?"

"I don't know any more, except the Crimea is over in Russia somewhere." Patrick wondered if he should have told her. But how could he have kept what he knew to himself? He wished that he had not known anything at all, that he had closed his ears to all the gossip.

"I had better take you back. Mrs. B will want to lock up," he said. He felt a little cooler and cast a glance upward. "Look, it's going to rain."

"Oh, yes," she said. "I have to get back afore nine. And get up in the morning and light the fires. Ugh! Such drudgery! But - but maybe not for much longer, Pat, for if my relatives are rich…"

"I don't want you to be disappointed, Emmy," Patrick said quietly, squeezing her fingers tightly.

"Oh, but I am going to find them," she said excitedly. "And do you know somefink, Pat? I won't take no for an answer from them. I will do it for us. It will be for us. Won't you be pleased, Pat? They will set us up in a good 'ouse, and give me my due. They will get you a better job, in an office or somewhere nice! You can leave the foundry then."

"I didn't know you had a problem about me being in the foundry," Patrick said quietly.

"Oh, I didn't. But now that we're ridin' in the world, I'm sure you won't want to work such long hours, and it's so noisy, you said that yourself. Don't be cross, Pat." She snuggled into him, and he was mollified a little.

But she prattled all the way back about her supposed relatives, and Patrick felt that she was in another world. Heartache was ahead; he felt it, saw it coming like the clouds rolling in now for the thunderstorm that soon broke over their heads. Heartache for her, and he would have to comfort her when she was coldly rejected, as he knew she would be.

But Patrick did not think ahead as to how some of those clouds might break over his head also.

THE LETTER

It took Emma a little time to decide the best approach to her relations in Belgravia. Should she send them a letter, or just turn up at the door? She remembered how rude the butler had been, and she carefully crafted a letter to the people she felt must be her grandparents, bypassing the butler and informing them directly as to the relationship with her.

First, she took an omnibus near to Elizabeth Street and walked past the house. She thought she recognised it by its blue door, but just to be sure, she went even closer and saw the number eleven on the plaque. Then she asked someone on the street who looked like a servant if the Lees lived there.

"The Leigh-Donners live there," said the servant, and walked on.

She did not know anything about the Donners, so she simply addressed her letter to the Lees.

Dear Curnel and Mrs. Lee,

You will be sprised to hear from me, Emma Lee, after all these years. I know you gave me to the Enrights to foster. They are dead now. I want to come to you. I am 17 years old now. Please send a letter to me at 86 Norland Square, Kensington, where I am risiding at present. Yours sinserley, Emma Lee.

When the letter was delivered the morning after she posted it, it was taken to Mrs. Leigh-Donner with her other post. She was now a widow. She was breakfasting with her second son, Wesley, and his wife, who had come to live with her.

She smiled ruefully and shook her head when she saw the poorly addressed envelope.

"A begging letter. Another widow of someone who was under your father, I'm sure. Look at the spelling of colonel, God help us. And 'Lee' instead of 'Leigh,' and no Donner at all. It's the worst I've seen; usually they do try to get the name correct!" She took up her little decorative knife and slit the envelope open.

As she read it, the colour drained from her face. She put her hand upon the ruffle at her neck and uttered a faint exclamation.

"What is it?" Wesley took the letter from her and read it, frowning.

"I thought all this was over and done with!" he stuttered.

"As I did! As we all did!" She seemed to choke on the words. "What shall we do, Wes?"

"What is this about?" Wesley's wife asked. She, too, took up the note.

"I never heard anything of this!" she said, amazed. "Wes, pull the bell for your mother. She is about to faint."

"No, I am not!" Mrs. Leigh-Donne rallied. "She calls herself a Lee. Could it be that they told her that is who she was? I must visit Charlotte this morning. I am quite well, Wes, thank you. This has to be dealt with for once and for all, and it will be my duty."

CHARLOTTE'S SOLUTION

Charlotte was surprised to see her mother-in-law so early in the day, for it was not yet ten o'clock. She was given the letter to read.

"Those conniving people!" was her exclamation. "They took the money, and told her that she was one of us! What treachery! That was not what was intended. But I knew I had to beware, some years ago when he brought her here!"

"What money? And I never heard about any. Is it here!"

Charlotte had to admit now what she had not told her parents-in-law at the time, about her arrangement with the Enrights to take the child Emma.

"But, Charlotte, you sending a remittance was like admitting responsibility!"

"I know that now, Mother," was Charlotte's miserable reply. "And when George put a stop to it, Jack Enright brought her here. But he never mentioned that they had used the name Leigh, or L-E-E as she spells it, for her. Artful people! No doubt they did not want the disgrace upon their own heads!"

"Artful indeed! What do we do now, Charlotte? If we do not respond in some way, she will turn up at the door."

"I beg you do not enter into any correspondence with this person, Mother. On the memory of poor Cyril, promise me you will not."

"I cannot promise any such thing! She expects an answer! Common politeness demands that at least."

"Then use an attorney, Mother."

There was a pause.

"Please, Mother? A letter with a letterhead from Messrs. Hothershall & Greybald ought to frighten her, to put an end to this once and for all."

"I doubt she is any threat to you now, Charlotte, but since you feel so strongly about it, I will do as you wish. It is a great pity you took the course you did, in sending them money."

LEGAL LETTER

Emma waited for five days before she began to despair of a reply. Then a full week later, the butler, Mr. Hensley, called her to his pantry in the middle of the morning. Mrs. Bowles was there with him.

"We have received a letter for you, Emma, from Messrs. Hothershall & Greybald, Attorneys at Law," he said, holding it in his hand and staring at it and at her by turns.

She looked as astonished as he had when he had seen the direction to Miss Emma Lee on the long white satin-bond envelope.

"I hope you are not in any trouble, Emma," Mrs. Bowles said to her sternly. "In all my years here, we have never received a letter from any attorney for a parlourmaid."

"I'm not i' troubl', honest, I'm not."

"Would you like me to read it to you?" Mr. Hensley asked, thrumming his fingers lightly upon it.

"No, thank you."

"Are you sure? Lawyers tend to use very long words that most people, even those with education, cannot make out."

"No, thank you."

"Were you expecting such a letter, Emma?" Mrs. Bowles asked.

"No, yes, I mean, yes, I was expecting a letter."

There was an awkward pause. She thrust out her hand suddenly, and Mr. Hensley put it reluctantly into hers. She put it in her pocket.

"Go back to your duties, then," Mrs. Bowles ordered.

After she left, Mr. Hensley's brow creased in annoyance.

"Mr. Greybald is a friend of Judge Carmichael," he cried. "What could he have to say to a parlourmaid?"

"I will get it out of her if I can."

Emma was very glad to leave the room and the disapproving butler and housekeeper. She trembled all over, and she bore the precious letter outside to the yard, hiding around a corner to open and read it.

Dear Miss Lee,

We have been instructed by our clients, Mrs. Leigh-Donner and her son Mr. Wesley Leigh-Donner, to write to you in reply to a letter sent to them by you dated October 2nd inst. Our clients are very sorry, but they are at a loss as to the connection you claim, and are quite certain that they have never made your acquaintance. Furthermore, the persons you reference in your missive are unknown to them. They are sorry if you have laboured under a misapprehension concerning a familial link, and ask us to inform you that there is no such link. They consider the matter to be closed, and wish you well for the future.

It was very hard to make out; Mr. Hensley was correct, but with the phrases "very sorry," "never made your acquaintance," "such link," and "closed," all was clear to her. They did not wish to know her. She burst into sobs, but then she remembered that she was expected back in the house; the parlour had to be cleaned. It was not fair! She could not even have the luxury of mourning her great trouble! Miss Clara had lost her kitten and had cried for two hours upon the couch. She could not even cry for her lost family.

She worked the remainder of the morning in an unhappy trance, her face drawn in sadness. Handling the precious items today was more bitter than ever. She was gentry, and that was why she resented being a servant. It was in her blood. The other servants were content enough with their lot. Service was in their blood. It was not in hers.

She hated being a servant. She should be wealthy. She should have everything the misses of the house had.

She wondered what to do next.

DUDLEY POND

Mrs. Bowles tried her best to pry, but was unsuccessful. "It was noffink," Emma answered her. Considering that she was the person now responsible for her, she thought it her duty to write to Mrs. Moore and tell her about Emma and the mysterious letter. When Patrick heard of it, he knew exactly what had happened, especially in the light of Mrs. Bowles saying that Emma must have had bad news, for she was unhappy about something, but was silent on the matter.

"I tried to tell 'er, Ma." He told his mother about Emma's intentions. Mrs. Moore did not wish to tell Mrs. Bowles what it was about. It was far too peculiar and might cost Emma her place.

I think it had something to do with her uncle's will. Mrs. Moore wrote back. *She was expecting something. But other relatives got it all. It was not much, but meant a lot to her.*

This cut no ice with Mr. Hensley, to whom the letter was soon revealed by Mrs. Bowles. A family from Whitechapel engaging Messrs. Hothershall & Greybald to draw up a will for a few old pieces of furniture and pots and pans? Not likely! He felt it incumbent to reveal all he knew to Judge Carmichael.

The judge was intrigued. He said it to his lady, who was as astonished as he.

"I pray you will ask Mr. Greybald," she said. "This is very unusual!"

"Greybald is as tight-lipped as a corpse about his clients, but a few coins to his secretary will do the trick," said the judge, and he found out the very next day.

He regaled his family that evening in the drawing room when no servants were present. Everybody found it very funny. What a joke! Emma Lee! She was a pleasant enough girl, very respectful, but one could never call her light-hearted. She looked quiet and serious. But not a word to old Hensley; he wouldn't tolerate those kinds of ideas in a servant.

"She is a good, efficient parlourmaid," Lady Carmichael said. "I'm not going to dismiss her. Pray do not tell Mrs. Bowles either."

Their son Rupert had a friend visiting for Christmas. His mother did not like him; he had ruined some poor girl in Chelsea when he had visited a house there, and should never be admitted to any society as a result, but Rupert, home from Oxford, and apparently unaware of his friend's disgrace, had brought him in tow, and they could not send him away. His name was Dudley Pond, and his hostess quietly formed the habit of turning up in the same room whenever he had an opportunity to address her eldest daughter. Pond was undaunted and remarked in letters to his friends that he had never seen such a plain girl in his life. The maids were much prettier. There was one in particular he would like to know better, and it would be quite a joke to make her fall in love with him, for Rupert and his family had come to know that she thought she was related to the Leigh-Donners of Belgravia, that staunch military family whose great-grandfather, a brigadier general, had been a personal friend of the Duke of Wellington. She was not a smiler, and it would be a joke to disarm her of her serious face. His friend wrote back and proposed a wager, ten pounds if he could make her his before he left town in the spring. He accepted the wager and set about his seduction of Emma Lee.

"FORGET ABOUT THEM EMMA!"

Patrick went to see Emma every Sunday afternoon. Sunday was a little more leisurely for the servants, for routine cleaning and polishing belonged to the other six days. After lunch had been served and the dining room set to rights again, she could take a few hours off. Mrs. Bowles liked young Mr. Moore and had no objection to followers if they were of good character.

Patrick waited for her at the railings at street-level. He gave her a quick kiss, for they were in public, and they began their walk.

"Where shall we go today?" he began. "I was thinking we could get an omnibus and go round by Buckingham Palace, as far as Trafalgar Square. Any news, Emma?"

She told him, sadly, of what had transpired, and gave him the letter to read.

"It's not so bad," he advised her after she had unburdened herself of her bitter feeling. "Forget about them, Emma. We'll go on as before. I love you, my family loves you, and you'll be one of us. You always have been, in a way."

"I've always looked on your family as my family. There! It's all planned out by God, and He knows best. These people in Belgravia, they sound like they are not nice people anyway, to 'ave sent you such a cold, distant letter."

"True! I know I wouldn't like 'em. To think that they could not sit down and write a letter to me in their own 'and, but get their lawyer to do it, and have it done so stiff and so cold. It quite frightened me. Oh, but I do so dislike the work, Pat. I'm not cut out for it. I wonder if I shouldn't prefer to be in a factory, but I'm afraid of offending your mother, so dear and sweet she is to me!"

"Tough it out for another year," Patrick said. "And then we'll marry. We can live with my mother and father for a while and save."

The prospect of a cosy home with the Moores, in the centre of their warmth and acceptance, pleased Emmy.

"But," Patrick went on, "you might 'ave to find a job for a bit, to 'elp out, so we can save as much as we can before we - before we 'ave a family. Then you can stay at home of course, an' I do 'ope there'll be the patter of tiny feet in our house, don't you, Emma?"

"Of course I do," Emma said warmly, thinking back to the time when she had held the youngest Moore in her arms. "I always wanted a family, Pat. I want at least four, two boys and two girls! But where could I work in Whitechapel, Pat? I don' like bein' in service."

"There's a new ship's biscuit factory opening soon. You could try for that, and 'and in your notice to the Carmichaels as soon as ever you can, so you can be nearer to all of us."

It was also in Patrick's mind that Emma was unsettled when she worked among the rich. It reminded her of what her life could be like if the Leigh-Donners had not dispatched her to Whitechapel. It would be better if she lived and worked among the class that she had known all her life.

"'rri'ht - I'll 'and in my notice then," Emma said, a little relieved to leave the exacting Mrs. Bowles and the spoilt Misses.

"That's settled then," he said brightly. "No more tears, no more wishin'. No more Belgravia or Norland Square and silver plates and toffs. Look, they're changin' the guard at the palace."

"Imagine livin' in a palace, Pat! They 'ave the best of everything! I wonder if the Leigh-Donners ever were in Buckingham Palace."

They soon reached the square and watched the children with their nannies feeding the pigeons, then they wandered over to the embankment to see the new gardens. Patrick noticed that while his eyes were upon the plants and trees, Emma's were upon the fashionable ladies walking there with their parasols.

The sooner she left Norland Square and the rich area surrounding it, the better.

MR. POND'S WAGER

Is that blighter lookin' at me again? It was not the first time that Emma became aware that Mr. Dudley Pond was staring at her. This time, she was in the hall waxing the banisters when he passed by, and she felt his eyes upon her. His steps slowed as they approached her, and only an impatient shout from Master Rupert at the front door made him hasten them.

I'm imaginin' things, she told herself. But she was conscious of being admired, and by a toff too. She was pleased at the thought, but then shooed it away. She was in love with Patrick.

She had a half-day every two weeks on Thursdays, and she usually went shopping, boarding an omnibus to take her wherever she wished to go. Patrick worked every day except Sunday, so she could never see him at that time. Sometimes Mrs. Bowles asked her to do an errand and paid her for it. It was an easy way to earn a little more money and enjoy herself too by taking an omnibus ride and going into good shops in the West End to admire the merchandise and dream that one day she would own things like that. But she was supposed to put all of this out of her head. She was engaged to Patrick, and her future was in a modest apartment in Whitechapel and buying goods from its many shops there, cheaper and of lesser quality, and from markets and stalls, and a lot of mending and making do.

She boarded the omnibus to take her to Bond Street, and as she took her seat, found that she had been followed by a gentleman who sat down opposite her.

"Miss Lee, is it not?" It was Mr. Pond, and he inclined his head in a sort of bow.

She blushed. Why was he here on her bus? Was he paying addresses to her? He looked very well turned out, wearing a blue coat of good quality, a white shirt and grey silken cravat, a black hat well-brushed, and shiny black shoes. He had a neat beard, waxed moustache, and carried a cane as all gentlemen did. The passengers stared, for upper class men did not usually use public transport.

"Mr. Pond," she answered him faintly, casting her eyes out of the window.

"What a coincidence! Where are you going, if you do not mind my asking?"

"I'm on my way to Bond St," she replied haughtily.

"But of course, how could I not have thought so. You shop in Bond St. Another coincidence. I am bound for Bond St myself!"

He had dark hair and steel-blue eyes and was handsome, and very skilled in the art of charm.

"Would you do me the honour of allowing me to accompany you?" he asked her, with another humble bow of his head.

"Mr. Pond, I don't fink that would be -"

"Excellent!" he said, not listening. "Now, we shall get off a few stops from here, at Knightsbridge, for I know a patisserie where we can sit and have a talk. I have something very important to relate to you, you see."

"Me? Why?" What is a patisserie, she asked herself. It was not like anything she had ever heard of before. Was it a sort of bench, or alcove? Should she be suspicious?

"You will see," he said with self-importance. "But it is vital I impart certain information to you personally, and I beg your attention for at least a short while."

She assented, curious and somewhat alarmed. They alighted near a small park, and he suggested they walk across it to get to the patisserie, whatever that was. There had been a hard frost. Traces of it lingered on the grass and the shrubs, but the sun shone thinly through the trees. The noises of the busy streets seemed far away.

"The path may be slippery in places. Perhaps you should take my arm," he offered.

She hesitated, but took it. She hoped that nobody who knew her would see her arm-in-arm with a gentleman, but that was unlikely. There were very few walkers today. She felt very ill-dressed to be upon the arm of a gentleman like Mr. Pond, with her cloth gloves mended none too well at the tips of the fingers.

"What do you wish to tell me?"

"It is this. I have been observing you narrowly."

There was a pause; Emma did not know what to make of it. She felt a little insulted.

"And I have come to a certain conclusion," Mr. Pond said with a sort of triumph. "Which confirms what I have been informed of you!"

"What conclusion? What were you told about me?"

"Permit me if I speak frankly. You are not of the servant class. There! I have said it, for good or ill. Do not be cross with me; I could not bear it!"

"How do you know this?"

"You have an air only seen in the well-bred. The way you walk so gracefully, and pick up things, like the poker, the forks, and spoons I have seen you do, delicately, with a gentility not seen in servants. You are a lady."

"You 'ave been very noticin', sir!" she said warmly, but she was secretly astonished.

"It is not just observant, but I am possessed of a certain knowledge of your true family, but first, I ought to confess, though it puts my heart at risk in a very dangerous way, why I speak thus to you, why I have a great desire to see you lifted out of this situation. I find myself with the tenderest feelings for you. I love you."

"Luv me!"

"Yes, do not think that a servant's apron and ridiculous cap can make you into some unnatural being without beauty or shape; I see it well enough, and I am smitten. My darling, may I address you so?" He stopped, took her hand in his, and kissed it over and over.

"Mr. Pond!" She withdrew her hand very quickly. "I oughter tell you that I'm engaged to be married!"

A disappointed, unhappy countenance was the consequence of these words. "I'm sorry," he said. "I am out of luck then, and should never have spoken. How ill-mannered of me! What rotten luck I have, too! May I ask who your intended, the lucky man, is?"

"His name is Mr. Patrick Moore."

"And what does he do, this Mr. Moore?"

"He works at Hodges Type Foundry."

"As-?"

"As a caster."

Mr. Pond sighed. They had almost reached the opposite gate and the patisserie. He said no more, was vexed, and did not know how to proceed. It was a complicating factor, one he had not anticipated.

"You could do better," he said at last. "A great deal better, and as a friend, I can tell you that. You are young, Miss Lee! I pray to know your age. I shall tell you mine. I am twenty."

"I'm seventeen, and I can't do better than my Mr. Moore."

"Such a beautiful age, but too young to be married and living in what will most likely be straightened circumstances, for a mechanic cannot make a good living. Is he the first man you have ever liked?"

"Yes, and the only one I will ever like."

"I cannot advise you, Miss Lee. For it is none of my business, and I must conceal my afflicted heart as best I can. But I feel it incumbent to tell you my opinion. Come, let us go in here, and we shall sit in this little corner, where I must impart some advice. Two coffees, Monsieur, and two almond croissants. Have you ever tasted an almond croissant? No? Oh, you will like it very much!"

They were seated. Emma felt very uncomfortable, as if she were being disloyal to Patrick. She looked with suspicion at her companion, and seeing this, he laughed.

"There is no need for unease, Miss Lee. Do you know, when I say your name, I see it in my mind as 'L-E-I-G-H? Leigh-Donner, is it not?"

She was speechless. The coffee arrived, very strong, hot, and creamy, and the conversation paused while it was served.

"How did you know?"

"It is known in society that they have severely neglected a family member for fear of scandal. It is bad of them, I think. But I am sure I can help you."

"I don't want to know them, Mr. Pond. Mr. Moore and I decided -" The croissants arrived, dripping with butter, and filled with sugared ground almonds, and she had never tasted anything as good in her life. She had never been in a patisserie before. This was a new world, and this *mossyure* chap bowed to her as well as to Mr. Pond. Nobody had ever bowed to her before.

Mr. Pond began to speak again.

"Perhaps you do not want to know the Leigh-Donners, but you have rights, and they have obligations. You need never meet them, you know, but it is only just that they should pay you an allowance, a generous annuity, for the rest of your days, to see you without worry for the rest of your life. Mr. Moore would be an even luckier man than he is now."

She considered this as her heart beat faster. Could this matter be resolved? Was it a mistake to let it be? Could she and Patrick buy a nice house with a garden? This annuity could mean that he could leave the foundry also, but only if he wished to, of course. Perhaps he could buy his own foundry!

"What should I do?" she asked, finishing her croissant and licking the last of the crumbly, sugary goodness from her fingers. It had been heavenly.

"Did you enjoy the croissant?" he asked.

"Oh, yes. I did so enjoy it, Mr. Pond. Thank you very much."

"What about a smile then, Miss? I haven't ever seen you smile."

"Is that why you brought me this croissant?" She felt amused; a smile spread over her face.

"Dimples!" he said. "Oh my, they should be displayed more often! I envy Mr. Patrick Moore, I do, if he is treated to such delectable dimples. Now for the other business, meet me next Sunday afternoon and I will have made arrangements to push the matter forward."

"I'll bring Mr. Moore," she said. "We always go out on Sundays."

He shook his head.

"It would be much better not to involve him for the present. What I have in mind is a very delicate negotiation and he may say something to upset it."

"Oh! I doubt that, but I don't understand, I suppose, these things. Mr. Pond! What time is it? Mrs. Bowles will worry if I'm not back for supper, and I 'ave to get to Bond Street for 'er toothpick case! It's ready to be collected." She pulled on her gloves.

"A toothpick case for your housekeeper!"

"Yes, it is bejewelled but one of the stones came loose. It was a gift from our mistress. They do 'ave such luvly things-" She stopped suddenly.

"Allow me to be of service and accompany you, Miss Leigh-Donner. I assure you will get superior service with me by your side. Such is the way of the world. You will yet enter it, with all of its advantages!"

Miss Leigh-Donner!

A BIG PORKY

Dear Patrick, began the letter. *I am writing becos I can't meet you Sunday. I know we said leave the matter be, but I been offerd help from an unexpect sorce, a gentleman here, name of Mr. Pond. He says he can help get me an annuity, I think he called it, that they are obliged to, and he says the affair is known everywhere among the gentry and everybody think me used very ill. Fancy that! He will have news fer me Sunday. Its delicat so he said I must go alone. I trust him dont worry I will write to you Monday next with news. All my love and kisess- your dear Emma*

Patrick was annoyed and worried to get this missive. Who was this interfering Mr. Pond, and how did all of this come up anyhow? He resolved to go and see her tomorrow during his dinner hour, but she'd be busy then serving in the dining room, so he wrote her a quick, brief note:

Dear Emma, I'm surprised to get your letter with the news. For we had decided together, but it is your business I suppose more than mine. I do not like the sound of this man Mr. Pond. Who is he to interfere? Are his intentions to you honourable? I must come with you on Sunday. You must not be unprotected.

He received a reply by return.

Dear Patrick, yes, they are honourable. I told him I was engaged, and he said you're a lucky man, and you will benfit from my luck to, you won't have to work so hard, you can buy a foundry if you like to so let me do this, please dear for us, do not come on Sunday he said not to because as I sed before, its delicat he said. Love, Your Emma.

Patrick was more concerned than ever. Who was this mysterious Mr. Pond? He did not like the sound of him.

"Something out of order, Pat?" his father asked the following day. They were on their way to the foundry and Pat had not said a word. "A lover's quarrel, is it? Your mother and I see letters flyin' back and forth."

"She's still not over this business about where she comes from," Patrick replied. "Some gentleman has offered to 'elp her with it and it's dodgy. He's up to no good. I'm going to speak to 'im about her, Father, and warn him that if he 'urts a hair of her 'ead, I'll kill 'im and 'ang for it too."

"I hope it won't come to that," said his father mildly. "But you 'ave to wonder, Pat, if Emma is worth all this trouble? Now calm down, don't get me wrong, I can see by the look on your boat you've taken umbrage. Your mother and I are very fond of Emma. But if she 'ankers after the good life, better than what you can provide, she's going to make you un'appy. That's all."

Patrick was offended because sometimes he had had the same thoughts. His last meeting with Emma had reassured him, and now here he was, full of anxieties and doubts again. He would go this evening to the house and demand to see Mr. Pond for himself, and warn him that he'd have to reckon with him if anything bad happened to Emma.

But Patrick's plans altered during the day, for mid-afternoon there was a little stir at the foundry, and he heard a voice calling his name. His foreman Smithers came in and beckoned to him. He had a visitor.

Inside the big iron door stood a fresh-faced dandy with a gold tipped cane, looking about him with a superior air. Mr. Smithers hurried with a chair, and he sat upon it.

Patrick had been greasing the machinery and was wearing his long apron covered in streaks and splotches of oil. His sleeves were rolled up to the elbow, and his hands were as dirty as his apron. His brow held beads of perspiration, and he knew his face was none too clean, either, from the inevitable times he had drawn it across his brow.

The stranger was looking at him with curiosity.

"You want to speak wiv me?" Patrick shouted at him, above the noise of the machinery. He wiped his hands upon his apron. He knew who it must be, and felt hopeful. The man who was seeking him out was perhaps keen to involve him in his fiancée's affairs.

The dandy inclined his head.

"You are Patrick Moore?"

"Yes."

"I wished to be certain I have the right man. You are engaged to Miss Emma Leigh-Donner."

"Miss Lee. Shall we step outside to talk, sir? It's quieter there. You have not introduced yourself."

"Dudley Pond, at your service."

They stepped outside the large rambling building into the tannery yard. A heap of fresh animal hides stank beside them, the cold air hardly making any impact upon the smell. Mr. Pond took out his handkerchief, but the sprinkling of eau-de-cologne he had bestowed upon it that morning hardly shut out the obnoxious smell.

"Wha' is your business wiv me, Mr. Pond?"

"I am here to ask you not to stand in Miss Leigh-Donner's way of bettering herself."

Patrick was silent, deciding to listen more before making his remarks.

"She is one of a prominent family here in the city, and only waits to be acknowledged by them. I have a contact in that family who is willing to meet her and put forward a proposition, whereby she will find a path to her rightful place in society. Will you stand in her way, Pat?"

Patrick was silent. A hundred thoughts milled about in his head. This man was a fraud. This man was sincere. This man was in love with his fiancée. His fiancée was very much above him. Emma was his, no, Emma should be free to pursue her own course. And he could not stand in her way. No man who loved her could stand in her way in a matter of such importance.

"Is that the meeting on Sunday?"

"Yes. And I am here to ask you to stay away, for her sake."

"Why?"

The man said nothing, but his eyes said all as he took in his person.

"I clean up nice on Sundays," Patrick said with a little defensive sarcasm. "She must be accompanied."

"Mrs. Bowles, the Carmichael's housekeeper, will be present. We are meeting in a place of her choosing. The family has taken a keen interest in her, and I am a guest, and have been present at all of their discussions and conversations about the best course to take to assist her. I am also, perhaps, attached to her, a little."

Patrick's fist clenched by his side. A swelling anger threatened to do the upstart harm. He felt suspicious. He was stealing his love away, and she, innocent naive girl who had no experience of the world, was falling for it.

"If you 'arm a hair of her 'ead," Patrick said, his fist rising to the chin of that of his rival, "you're a dead man."

"Now, Pat, you intimidate me." The man smirked and turned smartly away, enclosing his nose in the handkerchief.

Patrick sent off a hasty note to Emma and put it in the evening post.

'Mr. Pond came to see me and told me that Mrs. Bowles is to go with you. Is this true? If he has lied to me, you will know what kind of geezer he is, and you'll avoid him like the plague. If he told the truth, then good luck my turtledove, I want the best for you, no matter what. I love you and always will. Yours ever, Love, Patrick

Had Emma received this note, her life might not have altered so drastically. But Mr. Hensley was getting tired of being postmaster to a parlourmaid, and to put an end to the love notes, he set it aside. He was not a messenger boy.

THE ACTOR

It was all a lie, of course. But fifty pounds hung on the success of this seduction, for more of his friends had bet, and he stood to collect from all of them, and it must not fail.

He would have to engage the help of a friend who did not have a dog in the race. Pip Mortimer was as amoral and dissolute as he, and he went in haste from the Type Foundry in Whitechapel (ugly place!) to Mortimer's lodgings at Hammersmith, in a very old house called Riversedge, but more commonly known as Mrs. Howards Lodging House.

Pip fancied himself as an actor, and if he had not been born above the profession, he was sure he would be receiving honours at the Old Vic, or so he told his friends, but the truth was that he was not very good, and was turned down for the leading roles he felt he deserved, while turning down minor roles as being beneath him. He lived off an allowance from a wealthy uncle in India, who thought he was studying at law, a quest he had given up two years ago. He lived in Hammersmith because it was cheap and near the river, which he found romantic, and to add to its charms, in the time of Queen Anne, a horrid murder had been committed in the very rooms in which he lived.

He found his friend's proposition very amusing. "Fifty pounds at stake! And you want me to impersonate a man named Leigh-Donner? Give me my lines! But leave the Carmichaels, and come and stay with me till it's done, for rehearsals will be necessary."

Dudley went back to Kensington and a few days later packed his bags. Even Rupert Carmichael was not sorry to see him go. He had a way of sneaking about that annoyed him. Yesterday he had disappeared for an hour, and the butler had seen him around the back door near the scullery. What would take him there?

They did not know that he had been waiting for Emma to emerge, and when she eventually did, he had a note to give her with instructions.

Take a cab to this place. Tell nobody. He had scribbled out the address and enclosed some silver coins.

"Are you meeting Mr. Moore?" Mrs. Bowles asked her pleasantly when she saw her coming down the stairs in her best hat and coat on Sunday afternoon.

"Yes, Mrs. Bowles."

"Tell him that I send my regards to his mother."

"Yes, Mrs. Bowles."

Emma hid her trembling as best she could. She walked a long way from the house before she dared to hail a passing cab. She showed the address, still trembling. They set off, and she looked about her at the strange part of West London she was passing through. There was nothing familiar about her to reassure her. They were getting close to the river, and fog descended upon them.

Now she could hardly see the definite shape of anything outside before it was swallowed by the pea soup. It was as if she were entering an unknown land and might never find her way back. Her hands clutched her reticule. Was she doing the right thing?

Don't be daft, she told herself, *it's London.* They went on for another twenty minutes before the driver turned off the street and went down a small, winding laneway. Emma became more and more alarmed. Finally, he halted the horses.

"Here we are, Miss." She got out and paid him, and he turned the horses with difficulty, went upon his way, and was soon invisible in the fog.

She was standing in front of a large, plain grey house at the very end of the twisted lane. There was nobody about at all. She could hear river traffic and birds very near, so the river must be only a few paces away, and not far away she could make out the long lines of what might be a high bridge. As she hesitated, she was seen from the upstairs window, and Mr. Pond came down to answer the door in person.

"Miss Leigh-Donner. How happy I am to see you." He took her hand, her hand enclosed in her best glove today, and kissed it. "I am very thankful you have come. You are alone?" He did not let go her hand, but pressed it to his heart.

She nodded. Her heart was hammering in her breast. What would the next hours bring? What enlightenment was she to expect, what revelation? She followed him up a dim, quiet carpeted stairs, expectant, enthralled, and terrified.

COUSIN MORTIMER

"**T**his is my new apartment," he said to her as he ushered her in. "I waited at the Carmichael's only until it was ready."

It was not as good-looking as anything the Carmichaels had, of course, but then they were very rich. Mr. Pond was probably not quite as wealthy.

"It's 'andsome," she said, liking all the same the good furnishings and the elegant lamps. She fidgeted. She was alone with a man in his apartment. It was not safe to be here. She should have insisted Patrick be allowed to accompany her.

"May I dare hope that someday, you may call this home?" Mr. Pond asked her in a humble tone. "Of course, for a Leigh Donner, it would not at all be adequate. I will confide in you, dear Emma - May I call you by your first name? - that when I turn twenty-one next year that I shall have some money come my way, by my grandfather. Then we, I, can buy a good house in the best part of town, in Belgravia, near your relations, if you so desire. I have often stopped to admire the houses at Belgravia Square. So tasteful, every one a beauty! There! I presume too much! You are spoken for! Forgive me!"

At this moment, Emma could not think of Patrick Moore. He seemed to belong in another world, a world she desperately hoped to leave behind her. She saw the appealing eyes of the man before her, gleaming as he gazed upon her. She was relieved to have to make no answer as the loud knocking of the front door seemed to fill the house.

Mr. Pond rushed to the window and peered out. "It is he! I shall return with him in a moment! Pray be seated, Emma." He left her and sped down the stairs, and in a few moments he returned with a young gentleman in tow, spare of figure but well-dressed and of elegant appearance, and introduced him as Mortimer Leigh-Donner, grandson of Colonel Leigh-Donner of Belgravia.

WHO WINS THE WAGER

"Is it really my Uncle Cyril's daughter?" The young man rushed forward and took both her hands in his, drawing her up from her seat. He did not seem to notice her poor coat, her inferior hat, or the frayed muffler about her neck, though she was acutely conscious of her appearance. He was dressed even better than Mr. Pond and sported gold cufflinks with green gems - emeralds? Poor Emma did not know they were merely cheap imitations borrowed from the theatre. He wore a flat cap with a green plume at the side and sported a trim moustache. Strange, but then it might be a new fashion. He made her a deep, sweeping bow with one arm bent as if holding his stomach and the other held out from his body with his cap in his hand.

"You are so like his photograph!" he said with a wondering and stupefied air. "My father, his youngest brother

Stanley, always said that he felt he was alive. He dreamt it, he said. But nobody believed him."

Emma was completely tongue-tied. No words formed in her head or her heart. This felt unreal, and yet it was happening.

"Let us take tea," declared Mr. Pond, and rang the bell. The landlady appeared. She was a woman of about forty, with a white mob cap and sensible grey dress. She glanced at Emma, seemed to frown a little, but assented to the request for tea for three persons.

"Do the rest of the family know of me?" Emma found her voice at last.

"Yes. My grandmother, the dowager Mrs. Leigh-Donner, laments that she does not know you personally, and wishes to embrace you before she dies. The remainder of the family are in the country, for it is still in the shooting season..." Here, Pip forgot his lines. Emma waited. "...they will not come to town for some months, but before then I shall inform them of you, and perhaps I shall take you to see them. Cousin Emma, it is my great happiness to make your acquaintance at last. My friend here, Dudley, is a smashing fellow, and we have him to thank."

Dudley smiled, simpered, and tried to look bashful.

"He is the best man in the world, excelled at everything at school, and has honours and awards for Rugby, Dead Languages, and Drawing Cows. He was presented to the

Prince of Wales once as the most distinguished pupil at school."

Pip was improvising and Dudley cast him a warning glance. Pip was over-stepping himself and he had turned up in that ridiculous Tudor cap instead of finding something modern. And the ridiculous bow! It was as if he were in a badly acted Shakespeare play.

"I merely jest," Pip said.

Emma was becoming increasingly uneasy, but told herself to be calm. After all, Dudley had been a guest of the Carmichaels, who were very good, rich people. There was no reason not to trust him.

'And only a few miles off my real grandmother is sat in a comfy chair, lamenting that she doesn't know me! I hope they take me to her as soon as possible.'

The tea arrived, and Dudley, his back to them, poured. She was unaware of his taking a vial from his inside pocket and pouring the contents into her tea before handing her the cup and saucer. He was taking no chances when it came to winning his wager.

Emma found her voice, asked her cousin all about the family, and received answers that popped into his head, none of them true. She finished her tea.

The trap had been set. It was getting dark, and when she realised that she was not to be taken to Belgravia today, she mentioned that she should be getting back.

"I will not hear of it!" Mr. Mortimer stood up. "No, indeed, you shall not go back to that place, and be a servant there! What shame!"

"But...where am I to go?" Emma felt alarmed; this was getting out of hand. "Are you to take me to my grandmother now?"

"Oh, I fear she is abed by now. She retires early."

"You shall stay here, with me." Dudley said. He signalled to Mortimer secretly, for there was more to be done.

"My dear cousin, I hear you are engaged to be married," Mortimer said hurriedly, then. "And your intended is a type-caster in a foundry."

"Yes," Emma said, a sudden yearning for Patrick's company seizing her. These men were strangers, and she wished to be gone from them now. "His name is Patrick Moore. His job is very important. He 'as to pour the metal into the type molds."

The men suppressed their laughter.

"But that union would be impossible," Mr. Mortimer had been directed to say next, his lip quivering, for he had difficulty controlling his amusement. "My dearest cousin, no Leigh-Donner should ever go so low."

Low! Emma did not think Patrick Moore low! But through the eyes of gentlemen such as she had before her, he was low indeed, and she looked away, not wanting to see Patrick as they did.

"It seems you must make up your mind, Emma," Dudley said quietly, in an air of great suffering. "The Leigh-Donners or Pat Moore. You may not have both."

"I'll ask my grandmother to give her consent!" she said.

"She it was who directed me thus. You are not to come into her presence engaged to anybody. She has your future spouse in mind."

"That's – that's not fair," Emma said, but she felt very light-headed. The room began to go around and around.

Her cousin looked at her full in the eye.

"There is a handsome swain here in this room who wants to marry you. How can you not repay such devotion? His family and mine are old friends. If you were to marry Dudley, the Leigh-Donners would take you into their hearts, and do all that is proper for a daughter of the house. Your rightful share of wealth, and a life of leisure with servants to wait upon you. That dreadful letter they sent would be a bitter memory to them. It was the work of the eldest son, only his. He is a greedy fellow. Your grandmother had no part in it. She is blameless."

"I must go 'ome! I must go…" Emma got up and immediately felt dizzy. Dudley sprang forward to catch her before she fell. He continued to hold her.

"I fear I'm ill," she said.

"No, you are not ill. You are overcome with the prospect of your future. It is ordained." Dudley held her closer.

"Will there be fires in the bedchamber on cold mornings?" Emma said, hardly knowing what she was saying, hardly conscious that Dudley was too near her. She wanted to tell him that she felt recovered now, but her words felt a little slurred. What was wrong?

"A maid to light the fire before you set your pretty toe upon the floor, and a hot cup of sweet tea before you even get up, as the Misses Carmichael have every day," Dudley whispered into her ear. "It will all be yours."

"I lay it all, and my heart, at your feet," Dudley whispered again. "But I cannot wait for an answer; you must answer me now. Emma Leigh-Donner, will you become my wife?"

"And I shall set in motion all that is necessary for you to be accepted in my family." Mortimer was very near also, talking softly. "My grandmother will be *jubilant,* my father will be *delighted,* my aunts and uncles *ecstatic*! Long have they all wished for this and spoken of it. You are coming home at last."

"But what is your answer to be?" Dudley kissed her forehead. This was not proper! She wanted to protest, but instead, a strange laugh came out, and it seemed that the laugh was not coming from her. Dudley spoke into her ear. "We shall be very happy together. The moment I saw you, I singled you out as my future wife. We are meant to be, you and I. We must not defy fate. You will say yes, will you not? I shall have a broken heart if you deny me. Do not deny me..."

"Your face, it's swaying to and fro, let me steady it." Emma laughed her unnatural laugh again as she lost her balance and Dudley held her even tighter. Now she was in his arms, being carried somewhere. Pip made a quiet exit, congratulating himself, and wondering again why he had been turned down for Hamlet.

Dudley Pond won his bet, and Emma, late that night after her senses returned, wondered how to tell Patrick that she was to marry another, for even though she had refrained from answering his ardent proposal, she had now crossed a line that she knew would tie her to Dudley for the rest of her life. She loved him now, she had to. He was to be her husband.

How could life alter so much in one day? It was impossible to go back to the Carmichael house now, and every link with her old life had to be broken directly.

WHERE IS SHE?

"Where is Emma?" Mrs. Bowles was annoyed. She had not appeared to serve dinner upstairs, and now the butler wished to lock up the house. "Something must have happened. I shall send word to the Moores if she doesn't come back in the morning."

Patrick returned to his dinner at Lilac Lane at one o'clock on Monday to hear the news that Emma was missing. He went straight to Kensington to the Carmichael house and found Mrs. Bowles, and to his dismay realised that the cad he had met had lied to him, for with a lot of shrieking the housekeeper told him she did not know what he was talking of, let alone that she was to accompany Emma somewhere yesterday. Mr. Hensley overheard, went to his pantry, and tore open the note. Having read it, he crumpled it in a shaking hand and lit a match to it.

Patrick demanded to see Lady Carmichael, who received the news with shock. It dawned upon her that Mr. Pond's sudden departure and the missing servant girl was no coincidence.

"We will do everything possible to discover them!" she said to Patrick, who was pale as death. He hurried back to his work to tell his father what had happened and to ask Mr. Hodges for leave.

Rupert, shocked and disgusted at his friend, made a list of their mutual friends, and galloped away to look for information. After some fruitless enquiries, he rode down the twisted laneway to Mr. Philip Mortimer. He denied any knowledge. He hadn't seen Pond for an age. Having no reason to suspect him more than any other, the young Mr. Carmichael went on to the next person on his list. He got no satisfaction, until he came to the rooms of a former friend of the dissolute gang, who took no part in their exploits, but heard of them.

"I heard of a wager only this morning, dishonest, disgusting, almost criminal in my opinion. Dudley Pond bet that he could seduce a maid from the house he has stayed in. He lured her to the apartment of a friend under the pretense that a wealthy long-lost relative was there to meet her, and it was done. He probably used a drug to accomplish his dastardly act. She spent the night there, and this morning he took her away to a hotel. That was evidence for his cronies; he won his bet. Fifty pounds all told."

Rupert rode home slowly, sick at heart. He it was who had brought Mr. Pond into his home, a man of dissolute morals and reprehensible character.

I can't tell Mother all that, he thought, or Father either. I will tell them that they have merely run away together. This business about the wager and the luring to a house must be left out. He found his key and pushed open his front door, but before he spoke to his parents, he found Patrick Moore waiting in the hallway, pacing back and forth.

"Mr. Carmichael, isn't it? I've already spoken to Lord and Lady Carmichael, and they told me to await your return. Have you found out anything? Tell me!"

"Mr. Pond and Miss Lee are in each other's company," he told him. "And I have not been able to find out where they are. They may even be on their way to Scotland."

"No, they cannot be." Patrick said firmly. "A gentleman does not marry a parlourmaid. Not even if the worst has 'appened. I fear she is being held against her will. Her last letter to me was filled with hope for our future, and I can't believe she'd throw it all away."

Rupert Carmichael felt more guilty than ever, but would not divulge all he knew. It was a dreadful betrayal from Pond. He felt taken in, humiliated, and stupid.

"I'm sure you will hear from her," he reassured Patrick rather weakly.

"If I don't, sir, by tomorrow's end, I'll return to ask your assistance in finding her." Patrick said. "She's been abducted, and I will go to the police. If it turns out not to be true, she 'as to tell me to my face that our engagement is at an end. I won't believe it any other way but that way."

Lady Carmichael called to her son from the drawing room. Patrick left and Rupert cursed as he threw his hat on the hall table. This good man had lost his love to a ne'er do well who used her and would soon discard her.

THE FAIRGROVE HOTEL

"Why did we move to a hotel?" Emma asked. "Your rooms were handsome enough for me."

There had been a group of young men sitting in the foyer as they had entered, and she felt their eyes upon them, and sensed a ripple of movement. One man groaned, another laughed, and another took out his pocketbook.

Then Dudley had registered them as *'Mr. and Mrs. Smith'* and the man at the desk looked snooty, as if he did not believe him.

When they had reached the room, he said he had forgotten something, went downstairs again, and returned in very good humour.

"Why did we move to a hotel?" she asked impatiently.

"I have a friend coming to stay in my flat, and I wanted to be alone with you, charming girl that you are."

Emma did not enjoy his attentions and endured them because she had no other choice now. He was to become her husband. She had begun to regret her actions and wondered how she had succumbed yesterday, and so easily too. She had not felt like herself at all after the tea; she had done the unthinkable. Something evil had touched her. But it was done, and there was no going back.

But she was to be taken to meet her Grandmother in Belgravia, and take up residence in her home, until she married!

"Oh, I say 'yes,'" she said.

"To what, pet?"

"To your proposal, of course! I remember I had made you no answer!"

"Oh, yes! Now that is wonderful, all my dreams come true."

"When shall we marry, then?"

If Emma had known the knavery in her lover's heart! He struggled for an answer.

"When your family have provided for you. You will need a pretty gown, and something for your hair, and a handsome purse of money."

"I hope Mortimer hurries it up, then, for I do not want to live in sin. When will he come? I wish I had asked him."

Then she thought that she would not be fit to meet her Grandmother Leigh-Donner.

"Dudley, I have no other clothes but these," she said ruefully.

"I will take you to a friend tonight, and you will be outfitted as becomes you."

That evening they set off in a fine carriage, and after some time disembarked. Emma was disturbed to see that they were in Whitechapel, in a street known to her, and at a premises where no respectable person entered, called The Pink Feather. It was a disreputable club, with girls hanging around the doors, and music coming from the back room. He ushered her in. There were couples drinking at tables, and games of cards, and drinking, and the women were garishly dressed, and many had their hair tumbled down. Dudley went to the bar and spoke to the woman behind it.

"Doris, I beg a big favour. Get this woman some clothes. She only has what's on her back, and she thinks she's my fiancée. As respectable as you can find." He winked and slipped her some sovereigns.

"Go with Doris. She'll see you right." Dudley ordered a drink for himself and went to a table in the corner.

Doris brought her upstairs and into a room where she rummaged in a large wardrobe.

"Somethin' for mornings. Evenings, here. These should fit. And you'll want bloomers, stockings and chemises, here." She threw a bundle into a carpet bag. "You 'ave enough. Come on downstairs now."

Emma did not think that any of them were at all nice enough to meet her wealthy grandmother for the first time. In fact they were all gaudy, cheap, and more suited to the women downstairs than to someone in her position. She should have gowns like the Misses Carmichael!

"Haven't you anything better? I'm sure Mr. Pond wishes you to put out the best you 'ave," she complained. She espied a blue velvet in the wardrobe and pulled it out a little.

"This for instance. This I would like. The white lace collar is the finest. This will do."

"Get your 'ands off that," said Doris. "That's my daughter's best gown!" She slammed the wardrobe door, almost catching Emma's fingers.

"I will tell my fiancé," she complained. "You 'ave not provided me with anything decent or respectable."

The woman just laughed. Emma thought her the rudest person she had ever met.

When Emma returned, she could not see Dudley at first. Then she espied him at a table beside a woman with cascading yellow hair who had her arms around his neck. She thought that he should have leapt up and away from her, but he was smiling. Perhaps he was too much of a gentleman to pry her arms away and was awaiting rescue, so she went swiftly to him.

"That will do," she said to the woman, pulling her off. "That's my husband-to-be and you keep your low-class hands off 'im."

There was an amazed silence, then laughter broke out. But Dudley was not laughing. Dudley looked embarrassed.

"You surpass yourself, Steely Eyes" said the woman to Dudley. "I must go and tell my little Dorothy that her Papa is getting married."

On their way back in the carriage, Dudley caught her arm in a vice-like grip.

"You are a fool," he said.

"Why?" Emma was taken aback. "What did that woman mean by her little Dorothy and her Papa? You are not a Papa, surely? And not with one of those women!"

"There are many things you do not understand, Emma."

"Don't call me Emma," she said shortly.

"Why not?"

Emma wanted to tell him that only people who loved her could call her Emma. People like Patrick Moore.

"If you're to marry me, you can't see that trollop. I won't allow it," she said strongly. "Let go my arm, you're 'urting me."

Dudley did not reply. Instead, he struck her face with the palm of his hand.

"You said you were in luv wiv me!" she said tearfully, her hand to her stinging cheek.

"You are a fool."

"Take me now to my cousin Mortimer," she said. "I have no wish to live wi' you before we are married."

"You're stuck with me. I am sorry I struck you."

Dudley did not mean that, but he wished to keep her from leaving him, for she could go straight back to the Carmichaels, and then there would be trouble. He had heard that they took the news very badly that he had wooed a maid, and should Emma be aware that she had been drugged, and if it should get to Norland Square, the judge could well get angry and the consequences could be serious, for even servant girls had rights. While he could not see the judge publicly disgracing him, the matter could be reported to his father, and he could be sent to the farthest corners of the empire, kept short of cash, and banished from England. His father could be very unreasonable at times.

"Do you luv me, or not?" she asked angrily.

"I love you. I told you that, and I mean it."

"And, we will be married?"

"We will be married. Come here, my love, and forgive your poor Dudley, I shall not strike you again."

"Another fing. Those rags that woman Doris gave me are not fit for any respectable woman. You're to give me an allowance, and I will get gowns such as are fit for my new station in life."

Dudley was surprised, but found himself agreeing to this.

"And don't you ever 'it me again."

THE SEARCH

Patrick took three days off from the foundry, grudgingly given by Mr. Hodges, the owner. It would be three days lost wages, and Mr. Hodges warned him that if he didn't return after the three days he would lose his job, for there were plenty more lads awaiting at the door to get in.

Not wishing his family to think ill of Emma, he put on a brave face. She was young and her head had been turned. He pretended not to suffer as much as they expected him to in the circumstances. They would think only that she had gone away to find her wealthy family.

Above all, they must never know that she had been ruined.

Patrick had returned to Norland Square to speak with Mrs. Bowles, only to find she had left. The cook it was who told him, quietly. Mrs. Bowles and the mistress had

had a serious quarrel, with Lady Carmichael blaming the housekeeper for not supervising her maids properly, and Mrs. Bowles retaliating that Lady Carmichael only said that to ease her own conscience about having a lecher under her roof. Mrs. Bowles had packed then and there and left.

There would be no more contact between the housekeeper and his mother, and it was just as well; the link with the house at Kensington was broken. It remained only as long as he was searching for his sweetheart.

Patrick had gone to the police, and a constable visited Norland Square, but upon finding out that the parlourmaid and the gentleman had apparently run off together, told Patrick that he was a good-looking bloke, there were other fish in the sea, and he wasn't to drown himself in drink, and now if he didn't mind, he had criminals to catch.

Patrick returned yet again to the Carmichael house; he wanted the list that Rupert had used in tracking down Mr. Pond and Emma. Reluctantly, Rupert handed it to him. Patrick then began his task on foot and by omnibus, his love for Emma driving him on. Would he take her back? Of course. All she had to say was that she loved him more than this other fellow, whom Patrick was sure she could not love at all. Her head had been turned.

One by one he found the addresses and called upon the young men, and insults, disinterest, or contempt did not put him off in the various places he found them, boarding houses, bars, and private houses. All denied recent knowledge of Pond and said that they had never heard of the young woman Miss Emma Lee. All dismissed him in impatient contempt. He was undeterred.

One or two secretly admired the solid, deep love of an honest working man for his fiancée, whom they knew had been lured and wickedly used. Those few began to repent their part in the nefarious affair. They had not thought of the servant girl as a person in her own right until they encountered the man who loved her. Those few did not want anything more to do with Dudley Pond or Pip Mortimer, and amended their ways, and even years later looked back in deep shame at their part in the usage of a poor young woman.

THE PARTING

Patrick had one last man on his list. He made his way through Hammersmith, and leaving the streets behind him, he wondered if he had lost his way as he was directed to the secluded lane with wild marshy vegetation on either side and the sounds of the river very near. He hoped that this was not the place that Emma had been brought to. There was no life to be found except the old grey house at the end of the lane, which to his suspicious mood, appeared to be watching him. His uneasy feelings grew. A maid answered his knocking and pointed up the stairs to the suite of rooms that was the address for one Philip Mortimer.

Mortimer opened his door to find a tall, young, working-class man standing outside.

"Yes. What is it?" he asked roughly.

"I'm searching for a young woman named Miss Emma Lee."

"I never heard of her," Mortimer said cautiously. "Who are you?"

"I'm her fiancé, Patrick Moore, and I'm looking for the man who has abducted her. He is your friend, and his name is Dudley Pond."

Mortimer thought this encounter would be rather fun to watch, so he said, "I think I know now who you are speaking of. Mr. Dudley Pond has a new companion, a young, fair-haired damsel, better looking than the average young woman around these parts, who used to be a servant. They are engaged." He said this to see Patrick's reaction, and he was disappointed. The honest face did not fall in sorrow as he expected, but it hardened.

"Dudley Pond is not going to marry a servant girl. That's partly why I'm lookin' for her. If he has used her ill, I'm going to make him pay. Where do I find him?"

"I believe they lodge at the Fairgrove Hotel in Distillery Road. I shall take you there!" Mortimer, not wanting to miss any excitement or drama, hastily got his cloak and plumed hat, and they set off into the gloomy fog, with his companion wondering at the curious dress of this fellow.

Patrick paused in front of the hotel. His heart was in agony. What if Emma did not want to be rescued? What if she had fallen for this cad? He had to find out one way or another where he stood.

As they entered the foyer, a couple was descending the stairs arm-in-arm. Patrick immediately recognised the coxcomb who had come to see him at the foundry, but at first, he did not know the woman by his side. After a moment he realised that she was Emma.

She was lavishly gowned in crimson satin. Her neckline was low. A garish jewel hung about her neck. Her hair was curled under her hat, which was a creation of feathers and silk orchids. Her gloves were to her elbows, and worst of all, her lips and cheeks were coloured with carmine. She did not see him at first.

"Emma!" he cried out, distressed at what he beheld, disregarding the curious glances his exclamation brought.

She descended the last few steps looking at her delicately shod feet, ashamed to look at him. But she had to raise her eyes at last, and then flicked them away from him, over to the other side of the foyer as if looking for something else to cast her eyes upon.

This pained Patrick and told him nearly all he wished to know. But he was determined to hear the words.

"Leave us, if you please," he said to Pond. The other guests were pausing to look at Patrick, the working man so out of place in the posh hotel foyer. The manager, who was welcoming the guests into the dining room, wondered if he should throw him out, but decided to wait a few minutes instead of making a scene.

Mr. Pond shrugged and walked away, flinging himself into a chair and taking out a cigar.

Patrick spotted a quiet area by a window. He indicated that they could speak there. He put his hand upon her shoulder, and she appeared to flinch very slightly.

"Emma, I must know, are you here of your own free will?" he asked her quietly.

"Yes, I am."

"Emma, I have one more thing to say. It doesn't matter what you've done. I will forgive you, I will forget it, and I will always love you. I will never remind you of it."

She looked down, and he could not read her countenance.

"Are we still engaged, Emma?"

There was a pause.

"Emma?"

She shook her head. "No," she replied in a low voice, but with a very definite tone.

The word, and the decisiveness of it, drove a poisoned arrow through his heart. He felt shattered.

"Do you love him?" he asked her.

She was silent. She still would not look at him. She twisted her reticule in her white-gloved hands.

"It's for the fine gowns and the carriages, is it?"

She looked about, not answering.

Patrick turned and walked out of the hotel.

Mortimer, who had watched the entire scene played out from behind the front door, for he did not want Emma to see him, was very disappointed that Patrick did not assault his rival, and went after him.

"I say, Pat, go back, call him out, and take him on."

Patrick was struggling to keep his emotions from overflowing in the public street.

"I say, what kind of man are you, to let him take your girl like that? I want to see you fight him."

Patrick turned and looked at him savagely.

"It's none of your business what I do, when I do it, and how I do it." He finished his volley by shoving him, and he fell in the gutter, and Patrick walked quickly away. He suspected that Mortimer knew a great deal more than he had let on, from his skulking about the door, a leer upon his face, and not wishing to be seen.

FOR THE LOVE OF MONEY

Emma did not enjoy the sumptuous meal set before her. Guilt overwhelmed her. She had died inside herself. She had not even been able to look at Patrick, but she had left him, Whitechapel, Lilac Lane, the Moores, servitude, and poverty behind her now, so she picked at the roast lamb with mint sauce, the buttery vegetables, and the scalloped potatoes.

"Perhaps you should have gone back to him," Dudley said.

"We're getting married, Dudley."

"No, we are not."

"You asked me. I said yes. You're bound to me."

"I am not."

"Was all that luv-talk just to ruin me?"

"Do not use that word 'ruin'. It makes me feel bad. But yes, I suppose so."

I have given up gold for coal dust, she thought to herself. *Here is a horrid, wicked man.*

"You are bad. I'll trouble you no longer; find Cousin Mortimer."

He feared a scene in the sedate dining room, so when they were upstairs later, he told her: "I fear I cannot find him. I have tried. He seems to have left."

"Very well. I'll go and see my relations myself, then. He's given a good account of me, probably. They'll make you marry me," she said with triumph. "They want a union between the two families; they said so."

"I'm not as good a catch as all that," he replied icily. "I'm a third son. You ought to go higher."

"You're a lot better than what I come from," she retorted. "An' I'm not going back down."

"You embarrassed me in the dining room, asking for croissants. Croissants are for breakfast, and it's unlikely they have them here. They are French."

"Maybe I 'ave a lot to learn, but so 'ave you, about common decency."

"Have you given any thought to the fact that if we were to marry, we would not be happy for five minutes?"

"I'll be 'appy with mint. I've never 'ad it and I'll never be without it again. If you throw me over, I'll find another."

He threw back his head and laughed.

"You are an ignorant girl. Nobody with money marries somebody without it. I wish you luck!"

"I 'ave money! My relations 'ave money! You 'eard Cousin Mortimer!"

"Oh yes, your relations," he said drily. He smirked. She wished to question him, but she was tired now. She disliked this man. Patrick had said he would forgive her. If only Patrick had money! Perhaps I can persuade my relations to accept him, she thought. She imagined him dressed as well as Dudley and Cousin Mortimer, and standing as Dudley was now, before the fireplace, his elbow on the mantelpiece and a cigar in his hand.

She could not imagine Patrick Moore lounging about and smirking at her like that.

RICH RELATIONS

"Will you come with me?" Emma felt some trepidation in facing her rich relatives herself.

"No, I shall not accompany you," he said lazily. He was seated in a chair reading *The Gentlemans Magazine*. "Go by yourself; I am sure you will do very well."

He had his own plans to leave this hotel while she was out.

"Oh orright then. But I'm a little bit nervous."

"No need to be. I'm sure they will welcome you with open arms."

"I don't know when I'll be back. They might want to keep me there for luncheon!"

"I shall expect you when I see you, then."

"Are you not going to see me down to the door and call a cab for me?"

"No, I am not. Ask the concierge."

After she had left, he leaped to his feet and began to pack his suitcase.

Emma's nerves rose as the cab approached the elegant part of the city. She told herself there was no necessity for nerves at all. Going down that laneway to the big grey house, that's when she should have been nervous enough to turn back!

She had chosen, after much thought, to wear a purple morning gown, with white netting on the skirt and jacket. The maid had helped her with her stays and the buttons. A white hat with purple ribbon, white gloves, and reticule finished the ensemble.

She was stared at by passersby as she alighted the cab, and she took it as a good sign. The last time she was here, she was a shabby little girl trotting by the side of her uncle Jack Enright. He had been turned away by the snooty butler, but she was confident that a lady would not suffer that fate.

It was an easy matter to find the address again. An old man opened the heavy front door.

"Good morning. I am here to see Mrs. Leigh-Donner," Emma began, taking care to speak like the Misses Carmichael, pronouncing every word.

"Which Mrs. Leigh-Donner?" asked the butler.

"The elder Mrs. Leigh-Donner of course." Emma replied, after thinking quickly.

"I shall take her your card, Miss." He held out his hand.

"I am very sorry. I have lost my card," she blabbed, losing her composure a little.

"What name shall I give to Mrs. Leigh-Donner?"

Emma had thought about this. She knew that she might not get past the butler by giving the same name by which she had written to them, the name that had gotten her a nasty reply from the lawyers.

"Mrs. Dudley Pond," she announced.

A few moments later she was admitted. In her own house at last, the house she had been taken to as a tiny child! Everything was rich, fine, and beautiful in the hall. How she wished infants could remember things! It was not as large as she would have liked, but the colours were pale and gave it space.

The drawing room she was led to was heavy with brocades and oak furniture, but a good fire blazed. She sat gingerly on one of the armchairs, remembering the other time, in another part of this posh area, when she had been eleven years old. She saw photos on the cabinet, a man in military uniform with a handlebar moustache. Was it her father? He had bushy eyebrows. Other photos showed family members of dark and heavyset complexions, but perhaps she did not take after her father's side.

The door opened and an old woman entered, leaning on a cane. She was accompanied by another woman, younger, dressed rather plainly.

"Mrs. Pond, are we acquainted?"

"Yes, Mrs. Leigh-Donner, or I should call you Grandmother. Cousin Mortimer told me you would expect me to call."

There followed puzzlement on the woman's face, and upon that of the younger woman, and a few hurried words exchanged, which she heard clearly.

It's not the Enright girl, is it? Surely not!

The younger woman settled the old woman down upon a chair by the fire and fussily covered her with a shawl, taking a seat close to her.

Emma was thinking quickly.

Enright.

"I have never been an Enright," she said. "I was known as Lee." She was trying to pronounce every word properly to disguise her accent. "But now I know it was L-E-I-G-H."

"We sent you a letter," said the old woman. "Did we not, Miss Wood? Did not Wesley send a letter?" She plucked at the shawl a little.

"Yes, he did, he did, Madam, that he did!" Miss Woods nodded with vehemence.

"Yes, I got the letter," Emma said. "But since then, I have met, become acquainted with, Cousin Mortimer and he has told me, informed me, that the letter that was sent was a mistake and that you, dear Grandmother, want me to come here and be part of your family, as I should have been since I was brought here sixteen years ago."

She noted a puzzled look upon the old woman's face and Miss Woods' eyes widened.

"Cousin Mortimer? Who can she be speaking of, Miss Woods?"

"I'm sure I do not know, Madam. There is no Mortimer that I know of in the family."

"Mortimer is the son of your youngest son Stanley!" Emma cried out.

"Who is Stanley? Where did you meet this Cousin Mortimer?" asked Mrs. Leigh-Donner.

"At the Pond apartments in Hammersmith."

"Pond? Hammersmith?" The old woman looked incredulous.

"Her husband, Mr. Pond," Miss Woods said. "She must mean her own home, which must be at Hammersmith."

"I must admit, we are not married. I had to say I was, to get past the butler. The last time I was here, when I was eleven, he turned us away, me and Mr. Enright. I mean, Mr. Enright and me."

Miss Woods had to repeat this astonishing admission to Mrs. Leigh-Donner.

"Not married, and you call yourself married? That is unusual, indeed! And what do you want from us?"

"Recognise me as your granddaughter," Emma said, quite simply. "I was brought to this house, and I know I belong here. I wish to live here and be a part of your family, which is my family. I want everything that's due to me as a daughter of this house."

"Oh, good grief." The old woman bowed her head and put her hand over her face. There was silence. Miss Woods simply stared at her as if she were from the moon.

"Well? What's the matter?" Emma found a catch in her voice.

"You are not from us," said the grandmother, waving her bony fingers as if waving her away. "My son died many years before you were born. You are not from us. Pull the bell, Miss Woods. She will be shown out."

"You're very much mistaken, Grandmother! I'm a Leigh-Donner, I've always knowed that!" Emma forgot her grammar.

"We sent you a letter, and that was the final word," Mrs. Leigh-Donner said. "We sent you a letter. Did we not, Miss Woods, send her a letter?"

"Ooh, yes, we did, we did, Madam, we did send a letter!"

The younger Mrs. Leigh-Donner appeared then, and having been told of the situation, brooked no opposition. Wesley's wife took her roughly by the arm and pulled her to her feet.

"Perkins! Show this pretender out, Perkins. Do not return here, Miss Enright. If you do, we shall call the police."

"You can't mean that! I'm not Miss Enright! I was never Enright! I belong 'ere! You can't throw me ou' on the street!" Emma was shouting now.

"Yes, we can, and never come back. We contributed to your welfare for long enough, and you're not even blood. You cannot come here and tell us you are."

"'w are you so blinkin' sure?" she screamed at them, her accent completely forgotten now.

"Because as Mrs. Leigh-Donner said, her son was dead several years before you were born," Miss Woods said with a sort of triumph.

"You don't even want to think your son was alive! And might still be alive! What kind of people are you?"

They had reached the hall door now, she was pushed out by Perkins, and the door slammed behind her.

She knocked and knocked for twenty minutes. Screaming and weeping, she sat on the steps. A male servant came up to the street from the kitchen and hurried away somewhere. He returned with a policeman.

"Desist immediately or I will put you under arrest for disturbing the peace," the constable threatened.

She gathered her purple skirts up and got to her feet.

"'Orrible, nasty people!" she raged as she hurried down the street, with onlookers looking on in amazement. "I'm well rid of 'em! I bet I belong to nicer people than them! Who wants their bees an' honey!"

VANISHED

When Emma returned to the Fairgrove Hotel, it was to be accosted by the manager as she crossed the foyer to take the stairs.

"I'm sorry, Mrs. *Smith*" he said, with a sarcastic emphasis, "you are no longer a guest. *Mr. Smith* has checked out."

"What are you saying? That I can't go up to my room?"

"We have new guests in number 22. I'll thank you to leave the premises directly."

"But where did my husband go?"

The manager smirked a little. "Your *husband*, Madam, left no forwarding address."

"He must have left a note for me!"

"No, nothing." The manager espied a group of wealthy American tourists entering the front door, and nodded to a junior to deal with this trollop while he rushed to greet them. The man took her arm roughly, maneuvered her past the staircase, he shoved her down a dark hallway, and pointed to a door.

"Off you go! Out that door."

"No! What about all my fings? My clothes? Everyfing!"

"All forfeited. Smith did not have enough on him to pay the bill."

"You stole from me!" But in another moment, she found herself shoved out the door and stumbling into a dirty side-alley. She tried to get back in, but the key had turned in the lock and the bolt driven home.

Hammersmith to the house by the river! Maybe he was there, gone home! She half-walked, half-ran there, through the fashionable Riverside Mall, and streets and roads that got progressively smaller, and finally the laneway. The landlady let her in, and she rushed upstairs. The door was swinging open, and all was gone except the bare tables.

"There's something very funny goin' on here," said the landlady. "That Mr. Pond came back, and before you could say Jack Robinson, he and Mr. Mortimer went off."

"This Mr. Mortimer. What is his surname?"

"Why it's Mortimer, did I not say?"

"I thought his Christian name was Mortimer," Emma said unhappily.

"No, fer his Christian name is Philip. What 'as been going on 'ere, Miss?"

"They made a fool of me," she said, and sobbed. "He made me think I was related to rich people, and they took everyfing I had!"

"Oh, come now, Miss, there's no call for tears."

"But there is! I gave up a very good man, a good honest working man, for Mr. Pond!"

"You didn't - you didn't -"

"Yes! Did I not say they took everyfing I had? He said he loved me!"

Mrs. Howard held up a vial that she had taken from her pocket. "I found this in the room. I know what's in it. He drugged you with this, put it in the tea I brought up, I'll wager. You're not fully to blame, dearie, though you should never 'ave come 'ere on your own! I did wonder when I saw you up there! For though Mr. Mortimer is a gentleman, he's an arty type, and very odd. I only kept 'im as a tenant because, well, some don't like those rooms, given that there was a murder 'ere."

"Mr. Mortimer was your tenant? Not Mr. Pond, then?"

"No, not Mr. Pond. I saw him come and go a few times."

"He made me believe it was his apartment and that we would live there when we was married."

"Scoundrel! How I wish I'd never laid eyes on Mr. Mortimer, but as I said, I can't keep people in those rooms, for they hear and see things of the supernatural, and that makes them uneasy."

"I 'ave nowhere to go," Emma lamented. "I gave up my situation."

"I 'ave a little room at the top of the house, you can stay there until you arrange something, and maybe help me with some of the housework in payment. No men!"

"I'm not that kind of woman. I was duped."

"Very well, dearie. I believe you. For these gentlemen are not good men. Find your way up to the little room upstairs. Then come downstairs and I'll give you some cleanin' to do. You'll need to take off those fancy things. I 'ave an old gown that should fit you, and an apron and cap. I'll never let that apartment to a single man again, from now on, I'll let to couples only. My other boarders are very good people, and no trouble."

The attic room was freezing, worse than the one at the Carmichaels'. She looked with disgust at her new attire, a servant's costume again. Would she ever get away from this horrid garb that stamped her with lowliness, cheapness, and scrimping? Within a half hour she was scrubbing the stone steps of the house, her fingers cold and numb, and bitterly regretting that she had ever left Norland Square.

Why had she not listened to Patrick?

She was grateful to have a roof over her head, but it was not exactly kindness that motivated Mrs. Howard. She needed a maid at that time. Mrs. Howard generally suited herself, and had she not needed a maid, Emma would have found herself homeless.

RIVERSEDGE HOUSE

The months went by, and Emma settled into Mrs. Howard's damp house as best she could. She was a maid-of-all-work. She was relieved to not be with child, as Mrs. Howard had seemed to expect it more than she did, and she had questioned her every day for weeks. She was not happy, but looked upon this period of her life as very temporary. A newlywed couple moved into the apartment, and every memory of the old occupant was gone. Emma had to go in and clean it, but Mrs. Ellis was a sweet young lady, and kind, and her husband very pleasant. Mrs. Ellis did not like the rooms much. She said she got an odd feeling there when she was alone, with nothing to look out upon but the brown water of the river, and she thought she was being watched by some unseen entity.

Hammersmith was a busy, growing district and Mrs. Howard warned her not to go about after dark. All kinds of people were out, thieves and brigands. The river was a very good place for thieves and brigands.

Emma did not want to listen to her. She felt that nothing worse could happen her than had happened to her already, and sometimes, wanting to get away from the house and needing some air, she took a walk after she had finished her duties. Sometimes she walked the back way from the house down to a little inlet where there were bullrushes and an area of deep brown mud. Barges unloaded there, but always at night. There were children there, too, mud larks who scavenged the area for dropped pieces of coal, wood, or anything they could sell or bring home to their families. Some of the children had no homes and lived on the edge of the mud, eating what they could scrounge, sheltering under an old, wrecked boat or wherever they could. Emma felt sorry for them. Why were they so stricken with poverty? It made her afraid. Sometimes she gave them pennies, and they were grateful.

One of them, a young girl named Matilda, or Tilly, had been a foundling who had grown up in an orphanage. At twelve she had been apprenticed to a cruel mistress from whom she ran away. Tilly scavenged for bits of iron and wood and anything that she could sell. Emma sometimes brought her bread. She felt that she and Tilly had something in common, for neither knew where they were from.

One evening, on one of her walks through the village, it began to pour rain, and she hurried to take shelter in the nearest shop door, pressing herself to one side as the driving rain was lashing the step. It happened to be a tobacconist, and the door blew open a little. She became aware as she waited there, her hood over her head, that there were two men speaking with each other inside, and that she knew one of them by his voice.

It was Patrick's boss, Mr. Hodges. She knew him from his visits to the Moore household, as he called in there sometimes on his way home to instruct Mr. Moore upon something he wanted done the following day, as he had to be away. Was he looking for her? She discounted the possibility.

Pressed into the wall as she was, they possibly did not see her at all, even if they had glanced at the door swinging open a little. The rain was hard and noisy, but she clearly heard what was being said.

"Why did you have to bring me all the way from Whitechapel? It'd better be important. What a day it is!"

"I couldn't trust Her Majesty's Post, could I? And I 'ave nobody to send at present. It's this. The Starlit ran aground, she's damaged, ripped open, on her way to pick up the goods. And ere's the thing. When they got her to dry dock and 'ad a look underneath, they found her boards rotted. She'll have to be broken up for scrap."

A groan followed this.

"What to do then?"

"We 'ave to get another! Will you arrange it?"

"That'll cost us, to buy one."

"We can take one from its moorings, but then we 'ave the owners looking, and the river police might catch up to us. Better to purchase one cheap and send it to Gravesend, for the goods are waiting there to be picked up, and the longer we wait the more danger of being found."

"Where is the merchandise now?"

"In a barn. The Growler said 'e had to pay a farmer handsome to keep it and keep quiet too."

"What is it this time?"

"Four bales of silk, six crates tea, five tobacco, an' some watches an' trouser braces the lads found 'anging in the cabin, for they were daring enough."

"Perhaps it would be better to take it by road."

"Hodges, sometimes you're stupid. Under a bale of hay, I suppose, that gets overturned on a rickety bridge."

Hodges. It *was* him, then.

"I'm not willing to shell out for a new boat. I was caught for the repairs of the Starlit and you assured me it was river worthy."

Emma could hardly believe what she was hearing. The rain ceased, and she hurried away, fearful she might have been seen. She came into Mrs. Howard's kitchen and blurted it out to her. She was knitting beside the fire.

"Oh, that. Smugglin'. I hope they din't see you."

But Emma had questions. Mrs. Howard told her what she knew of the river criminals.

"Perhaps a ship had run aground in the estuary, and while the Master was trying to get it floatin' again, it may well have been robbed by a gang who were always on the lookout. They 'ave it down to a fine art; sneaking up in 'umble fishing boats, young lads boarding and finding the goods, throwing them to the boats. All could be done in a very short time while the ship's master and officers are occupied looking down at the sandbank and wondering how to get off it."

Mrs. Howard chuckled then and loosened her stitches on the needle before turning it and beginning the next row.

"Relieving the ship of some of 'er goods might well get 'er floating again, and the Master thinking it was his own skills! The lightermen are sometimes in on it too and deliberately run it onto the sandbank, 'aving the lads ready to come an' get the goods."

"Lightermen?"

"Those sailors that know the estuary and are employed to guide the ships up. Pilots they might be called, as well. So after robbin' the ship, the small boats are rowing to shore or hidin' in a cove, the ship goes upon her way to London

Docks, and only there after unloading is the theft discovered. But it's too late then to do anything. The boats have long put ashore, and a coal barge or something similar sets off with the stolen goods well hidden. But isn't it curious that the man you recognised runs a factory. He was probably involved in this smugglin' before he started it, and would it not be too lucrative to give up? Something for nothing. Some people are always after it."

"I remember hearing he inherited the foundry. Mrs. Howard, should I go to the police?"

"Over my dead body! Do you want to be fished out of the river someday like a drowned dog? These men are thugs. They'll not give up their enterprise easily. Make me a cup of tea, Emma. I get it cheap, but don't tell anybody!" She winked. "My old man used to keep 'is eyes shut when 'e saw things going on in the river, an' we always got tea very cheap, and I'm still on good terms with a few people."

It troubled Emma that the Moores were working for somebody who was involved in crime. No wonder Hodges had a big house and two carriages! This was his main source of money! She voiced her concern to Mrs. Howard as they sipped their late-night cup of tea.

"The machine shop is his cover. Respectable man, with workers under him, manufacturing whatever it is he manufactures, metal type for printing, is it? Who would suspect him?"

She pondered it for a time, and even wondered if she should go to Whitechapel to tell Pat, but then she had something else to occupy her mind. Her own health began to give cause for concern. Her appetite had vanished. At first, she thought she was simply tired, but as the year wore on, it became apparent that something had altered.

DR CADOGAN

As Christmas approached, Emma began to feel tired and ill. She had rashes on her hands and feet that came and went. She had headaches and felt faint, and to her horror, clumps of her hair began to fall out. And yet sometimes, she felt quite well.

"Come on Emma!" Mrs. Howard lectured her. "If you're as sick as you say, you should go to the doctor. He charges a guinea. Sell that fancy outfit you 'ave upstairs."

Emma did not want to part with the purple gown and jacket, the gloves, or the hat. They were her Sunday best, and she wore them to church. She never heard the words preached from the Bible or the curate's sermons. Her mind was busy with other things. How to attract young men? The only way out of her drudgery was marriage, and marriage to a man who could afford a servant, for this bride did not wish to spend her life scrubbing!

Doctor Cadogan was a young man whose arrival in the neighbourhood had occasioned excitement, for he was single and good-looking, if not exactly handsome. He attended church and bowed to her a few times, evidently not knowing that she was a servant. She would consult him with her complaints, because how else were they to be introduced? She was confident that having made his acquaintance, he would wish to know her better.

Over the past year, Emma had been very prudent in money matters. She had pawned her good hat to buy poplin and sewed herself a blue gown trimmed with red ribbon. She had scoured the markets for old gowns that held the promise of new life if the good parts were cut out and sewn together, for a new gown could be made from two if the colours and fabrics blended well, and the joinings were trimmed with ribbon, nobody would be any the wiser.

Mrs. Howard gave her money to do the marketing, but she drove bargains and put what she saved away for herself to buy sewing materials, haberdashery, ribbons, frills, and ornamental buttons. She told herself that it was not wrong. She was merely borrowing it and would repay it when she was married. But she had to marry well. Dr. Cadogan liked her; she knew it, and she felt confident that she could trap his heart.

Dressed in her blue poplin, she went to Dr. Cadogan's surgery to consult him. She was gratified to see him flush slightly and rise to his feet as she entered. He did not have a secretary, and asked her for her name. "Emma Leigh-Donner," she said, spelling her surname. She would never use the name 'Lee' again.

"And what seems to be the trouble?" he asked pleasantly, indicating that she should sit down. She explained her fatigue and the rashes that came and went, though she hastened to add that her accommodations at Mrs. Howards were very hygienic. He palpated her neck for lumps, asked her to open her mouth and say 'AAAH,' listened to her heartbeat, and asked her more questions. When he asked her if her hair was falling out, she had to admit it was and show him. She had not mentioned that and would rather he did not know.

"I am afraid I am not certain of a diagnosis," he confessed to her at last. "I shall have to send you to a specialist."

"Oh, Doctor Cadogan! I must not! I mean, Mrs. Howard would be very alarmed if I were to consult with a specialist. I am companion to her and she depends upon me very much."

"Very well then," he said courteously and said that if she did not wish to see a specialist, he would consult with one and let her know his opinion.

"Thank you," she said, handing him a guinea, hoping he would refuse, but he did not.

"Perhaps I shall see you in church next Sunday," she said as she departed, with a little flutter of her eyelashes.

"Perhaps." He bowed and she left. He began a letter to Dr. Manners, a specialist he knew, explaining his suspicions to him about his patient. He then looked out the window for a time, wondering, and somewhat disappointed. He hoped he was wrong.

Two days later, a reply came from Dr. Manners.

"Your suspicions are most likely correct," he wrote. "But she must come and see me before I can be sure."

He called to Mrs. Howard's that evening. Emma opened the door. The December evening had closed in early with a heavy, cold downpour, and it was dark in the hall. She had been working hard, and a lock of her hair was hanging over her eyes. She recognised the figure on the doorstep by the dim light from a sputtering candle she carried and a carriage lamp he had borrowed to light his way.

"Oh - " she exclaimed, shutting herself up just in time. She was suddenly conscious of her servants' garb and smell of lye soap on her hands, but the darkness saved her, as he asked to see Miss Leigh-Donner.

"Ooh I'm sorry, she's out shoppin'," Emma curtsied, hoping not to be recognised, and using her very best Cockney in a falsetto voice.

"Please give her this," the doctor said, handing her an envelope. "Make sure she gets it."

"Yes, I will," murmured Emma, dying to shut the door in his face. He turned and ran away to his waiting cabbie who had refused to go down the lane in the dark.

That was very close, Emma thought. I don't want him coming here. She hurried to the kitchen and read the note. She was to see Dr. Manners before a definitive diagnosis could be made.

But there was one other thing she wanted to attend to, and that was to give poor Tilly a proper Christmas.

"Mrs. Howard, can we? She can 'elp with the serving." Mrs. Howard had some boarders who were staying for the season.

"I suppose she can," Mrs. Howard said carelessly. "I don't want her to think she's going to be paid, though."

"No, not at all. She can be 'ere to get some good food into her, sit with us around the fire maybe, and 'elp us out like I said."

"Oh, all right. I suppose it's no harm to do somebody a good turn at Christmas."

Tilly came with her pathetic box of possessions, and Emma made her welcome. She took an attic room even pokier than Emma's. Emma was hoping that Mrs. Howard would keep her on with pay for the harder work, and promote her, Emma, to housemaid. It would suit everybody. Tilly would have food, shelter, and a situation, and Emma would not have to scrub those steps anymore, which was the job she detested the most.

DIAGNOSIS

It was Christmas, and Emma had seen Dr. Manners three days before. She had not liked him, his probing was rude, asking personal questions about herself, like if she had lain with a man. He said that he would send his findings back to Dr. Cadogan.

Emma was worried. What could this be?

She went to church on Christmas Day, and her eyes sought the doctor. He was there. The jubilant prayers, the carols, the bright wishes were of no account to her; she wanted only to speak with him, for she could bear the tension no longer.

At least they knew each other now, so there was no impropriety in her approaching him after the service.

"Miss Leigh-Donner. Merry Christmas," he said, raising his hat.

"And to you, Doctor Cadogan. Would you mind if I walked with you a little bit? There is something very pressing on my mind, and your surgery is closed for a few days. I am every moment worried, distracted, and anguished. I must know what is afoot." Emma was careful to pronounce each word properly and speak like the Misses Carmichael. It was the way she planned to speak from now on.

"Let us walk, then," he said, somewhat reluctantly, and stepping out on the icy path. "And mind your step, Miss Leigh-Donner." He offered her his arm.

She was very gratified to be seen upon his arm! A courtesy only perhaps, but then, perhaps not. It would warn off some of the other hopeful girls to see a lady on his arm.

He led her through the churchyard because it was quiet there. There was nobody else among the gravestones.

"Miss Leigh-Donner, it is a matter of some seriousness. I suspected it, and Dr. Manners confirms it. You have been infected with a venereal disease."

"A what?"

"A venereal disease, a disease you got from a man."

"From a man!"

"Yes, and the man who gave it to you, got it from a woman."

Slowly, she began to understand. Horror and shame descended upon her. Her world altered in that instant.

"It is not what you think," she said to him desperately. "I was drugged with a vial of opium and was senseless!"

"It is indeed most tragic," he said. "And I would not have told you today of all days, a day which is meant to be full of hope and joy, but you were particularly anxious to know. If it is as you say, Miss Leigh-Donner, it is a matter for the police. He should be prosecuted."

Emma shook her head. To have to go to court, to give her testimony, for it to be in the papers, for Patrick to read it, it was unthinkable!

"Is there any cure?"

"Yes. Do you have any family, Miss Leigh-Donner?"

"No, I do not."

"The treatment will be expensive and will require a hospital stay, for it is a hard treatment, with mercury."

"Doctor Cadogan, I'm not a companion to Mrs. Howard. I'm only a servant! I 'aven't got nuffink!" Her cultured accent disappeared of its own accord, and she lapsed into Cockney.

"Oh." He sounded astonished. "I thought -"

"It was me who opened the door to you when you come to the 'ouse!"

"You? You were that maidservant?"

She nodded, miserable.

"I was born to a wealthy family, but they don't want me. It's a very sad story. I'm doomed to die, ain't I? I can't say I'm sorry. It might be the best fing."

"Miss Leigh-Donner, do not say that. You can be treated by the parish. Some of the hospitals, unfortunately, have ceased to take public patients suffering from this disease. In the last district I worked, I sent several poor patients to the workhouse, who have not reneged upon their duty in this regard, and hopefully never will."

"The workhouse!"

Aside from the disease, all of her hopes of self-improvement were dashed by being sentenced to the workhouse, the last refuge of even the poorest people.

THE FOUL WARD

She sold her good purple suit, for she would not need it now, and left the money for Mrs. Howard, who had not even been aware that she had been cheated. She wrote a note apologising for leaving suddenly. It was deeply shameful to have such a disease. And then she turned her steps toward Brickhill, where the dreaded building was.

The doctor had given her a note and she was admitted immediately. There had been a little argument at the gate with the porter. "We don't 'ave double-barrelled names 'ere," he smirked.

"You must enter my name as the doctor wrote it," Emma said shortly. Though she wanted nothing to do with the Leigh-Donners, she might as well keep the name, for Lee meant nothing to her, and she had never thought of herself as Enright. There was no law against calling yourself whatever you wanted, she thought with a little spite. Perhaps they might even hear of her again, and it would irk them no end to think she still had their name!

The section of the workhouse where she was sent to was called 'the foul ward'. Emma thought that it was called that because it was a judgement upon the sufferers. She and the other patients here were the dirtiest people in London and in the workhouse. It was a locked ward, for the patients were not allowed to meet anybody else in the workhouse. Not that they wished to; they were treated like outcasts and regarded with revulsion, as if they carried the plague. They had a small open area in which they could take fresh air, but it was surrounded by high walls. The men's foul ward was the next building and was connected to the women's ward inside by a long hallway.

She was in a world within a world, locked inside, with other poor women who were in the same situation as she. She looked about the long dark room like a deep cavern, with rows of beds crammed together and a smell that was a mixture of strong disinfectant and body waste, the former waging war against the latter. Except for a low moaning coming from a bed near the end, and an intermittent muttering, it was eerily quiet. As she was led down to her bed by the attendant, she looked at the other patients with a sense of dread.

This woman, bandages on her face hardly concealing the sores beneath - would she become like her? Or this thin woman staggering up the ward, gasping, holding on to each bedstead as she advanced? Or the woman sitting on the side of her narrow bed staring at her with wide, bitter eyes? Or this bedridden, moaning patient, drooling at the mouth, whose bed smelled? And another not in her right mind, calling out to Bill and Joe. Surely, she did not belong with these people!

"I'm not sick like these," she protested.

"Yes, you are," said the bossy ward attendant whose name she was to know as Mrs. Tupper. She was a widow, small and round like a barrel. "You've all got the pox one way or 'nother. This is your bed 'ere. Get in." Her clothes had already been taken away, and she thought, fumigated, for everything about her was considered dirty, and she was wearing a coarse cotton nightgown with stains here and there. How many other patients had worn this nightgown? Where were they now, those other foul people? The nightgown had worn threadbare from too many washings and the thin material left had acquired a smell. It was a penance to wear such a horrid thing.

She considered herself severely soiled in her mind more than in her body. The doctor had said her body was curable. But her mind, the bitterness swallowed her up; she was drowning in it. Every thought was angry, every feeling was harsh in self-condemnation. If Patrick could see her now, or his mother and sisters! How they would all despise her! Even little William would scorn to know her, he whom she had carried around in her arms almost until he could run.

She climbed into her hard lumpy bed and lay down. Her eyes took in the high ceiling above her, mottled with age, greyish and blank. Even if she lived, she was truly ruined. Having been here, was there any hope for her in the future? Only a few short weeks ago, she had hopes of Doctor Cadogan! He was almost falling in love with her. He might have married her, but for this!

But I didn't love him, she thought. *I wanted to be married to somebody who could afford servants.*

I deserve all this! I became mad with envy of people who had more than me, and then Patrick wasn't good enough for me. I put myself into danger when I went alone to the house in Hammersmith. He begged me not to! As for being acknowledged by the Leigh-Donners, what hope do I have now? Pat loved me. How I wish none of this had ever happened; I rue the day I urged him to tell me about how I was found!

THE PATIENTS

The days passed, and Emma's mercury treatment began. She had ointment rubbed all over her skin, and then had to sit in a hot room with the other patients to induce sweating. This surely could not help her! Why could she not take pills and go back to bed and sleep?

"No, they'll kill you quicker'n the pox," she was told by the nurse in charge.

She had only been in the foul ward a few days when she was alarmed to find herself approached by the woman with the bandages covering the visible sores upon her face.

"I know you. I've seen you before," she said to her. Emma looked at her aghast.

"I'm sorry. You're mixing me up with someone," she said.

"No, I'm not. You were wiv 'im too. Dudley Steel Eyes. You pulled me off of 'im. Remember?"

Was this the woman she'd met in that low-down pub in Whitechapel? The woman with the yellow hair? The woman seemed to know what she was thinking, because she pulled her cap off to reveal an almost bald head.

"Now put a yellow wig on me! Did you get the pox from 'im or from someone else?"

"There was no one else!" Emma replied indignantly. After a moment she added, "Did you get it from him too?"

But the woman said nothing, and Emma realised she had it the wrong way around. This woman had given the disease to Dudley. And remembering what Dr. Cadogan had said, this woman had gotten it from another man, who had gotten it from another woman, who had got it from a man. Emma began to feel sicker with each successive thought in her head. It was as if she had lain with everybody who had this disease since it began in somebody. She turned her back on the woman and wept silently.

Later, she remembered that this woman had a child. She found the courage to go to her and ask her about her daughter.

"I brought 'er to Steel Eyes, cos I thought he might've been lucky and escaped the pox, but I couldn't find 'im. I put 'er in here, in the children's section. She cried and cried, telling me she'd be good, she'd never be naugh'y again, poor girl! I 'ope she never finds out what I was and what I died of. Oh, my heart is raw with pain. I can't stand it!"

"But if you get better, you can be together again, can't you?" Emma said. "We will get better, won't we?"

The woman made no reply.

Poor unfortunate girl, Emma thought. Alone, motherless, fatherless. At least I had a home and a family life, she told herself, for the first time feeling that there were children who were worse off than she. This made her think of the Moore family, and their open arms. She wept more. Had she any tears left inside her? She felt drained and numb.

A week later, this woman died.

Emma felt unwell and continued to feel unwell for weeks as the treatment continued. The days were long and unrelenting. The atmosphere in the ward was gloomy and depressing. Everybody was suffering, either from the disease they had, the harsh cure, or memories of better times. She grew very despondent.

Some of the other women had tragic stories. Sophie was the wife of a weaver whose husband had been unfaithful. She had four small children, all now in the workhouse, as her husband was a patient in the male foul ward, and they had nobody to look after them. His lack of fidelity had caused disaster for the family.

Lily had been newly married when she contracted the disease. "I couldn't believe it for a long time," she said to Emma. "I thought the doctors 'ad made a terrible mistake. I thought they were mixing me up with somebody else. My husband killed 'imself. Worst of all, my baby was born with the syphilis," she wept. "He died after a few days. What 'appened to you? I know you're not one of those women." She nodded toward a little group who liked to keep to themselves. They were prostitutes. Sophie and Emma felt sorry for the youngest, a girl of only fifteen, though she looked thirty or more, with a lived-in face that may have never known the happiness of a real childhood.

Emma did not want to talk of herself, except to say that she had been tricked, and found herself alone with a man who had poured a drug into her tea.

"Only tha' one time? And you got this?" Lily was horrified, and a little disbelieving.

With a girl named Jenny, Emma was more honest. Jenny had had an affair with a married man. Jenny liked nice things, and he bought her fancy ribbons and hats. He was well-off. But he threw her over after six months, and here she was now. She felt she was being punished, as Emma felt sometimes. She was honest with Jenny and felt better for it.

"But if Mr. Moore loves you, 'e might take you back," Jenny said brightly.

"No, for he wants children, I know he does, and this treatment means I won't be able to 'ave any. He comes from a big family, and his older sisters already 'ave children."

"I do so like pretty things, though, is that a sin?" Jenny asked.

"I don't know. I know noffink about religion."

"My way of getting pretty things were a sin," she said ruefully. "I don't suppose I'll ever 'ave anything fancy again, not so fancy as Mr. Thorne bought me."

Emma thought of Edith, Sandra, and Frankie the footman, who did not hunger for expensive objects but wanted other things in life and were content to strive for what they could reach with hard work, wisdom, and patience. Why could she not have been as content as they were?

She had reached too high for the stars and taken a terrible fall. There were Christian quotations here and there in the ward, and her eyes tried to avoid them as much as possible. The one that annoyed her the most was an exhortation to 'Be Thankful in All Circumstances'. That sounded impossible here in the foul ward.

CHRISTMAS IN THE LEPERS CAVE

It was Christmas in the workhouse, and Emma had been a patient for almost a year now. The treatment had produced several nasty side effects, and she was feeling increasingly unwell.

At Christmas, the paupers at Brickhill Workhouse were remembered by their patrons, the Board of Guardians and their wives, and the charitable people of means in the parish, but the patients in the foul wards were forgotten. Nobody remembered the 'undeserving poor' who had brought their sicknesses upon themselves, or so it was thought to be. The innocent who contracted it from errant husbands and wives were not thought of. Most of the patients in the foul wards were guilty of sin. So they suffered with only themselves for company, and their attendants, many of whom had the same attitude toward them, and one or two of which belaboured them regularly for their downfall.

Most of the patients with 'the pox' did not wish for Christmas anyway. Separated from their loved ones, and not allowed visitors, they pretended it was just another day in the foul ward. But they did not have the ointment rubbed on today, and they were to expect a better dinner than usual, though few would be able to do it justice.

Feeling very ill, Emma lay in bed. Since last night, her stomach felt as if it were full of scalding water, her bones as if nails had been driven through them. She was burning up; perspiration poured from her; the sheets were wet, matted, and bunched, and her straw pillow so moist it felt like she lay upon prickly, wet grass. She shivered with cold one minute and burned with fever the next.

"Are you not getting up today?" Mrs. Tupper asked. She was one of the more sympathetic attendants, but she was easy-going to the point of neglect.

"I'm too ill. I won't last the day. I can't. Let me go in peace. How I wish for death!"

"You're that ill? You can't be. I don't want to call the doctor in, away from his Christmas dinner."

"Don't call any doctor. Just let me die."

"Are you as bad as all that?"

"I won't last the hour. Oh, dear Patrick! Where are you?" She moved restlessly about, agitated, in agony of body and mind, her mouth parched, yet the incessant dribble that was one of the curses of this treatment escaped the corner of her mouth onto the pillow.

"Get my prayer book." Sophie had come to her bedside and cried to another patient to do the errand. "Emma needs the chaplain, Mrs. Tupper!"

"The chaplain! I don't want to call the chaplain today. He's had a busy morning! He's entitled to his Christmas dinner in peace!"

Emma felt herself drifting into a deep sleep from which she hoped she would never awake. How welcome it was, with the scalding and the nails losing their power at last! The ward drifted away, the voices fading. Before night, she would be still and the porter would come with a stretcher to take her to the dead house, that shed at the back of the yard. There was steady traffic to the dead house.

"No!" she murmured. She did not want to be taken away in death and lie in the dead house. "No, help me, God help me!" She was screaming now.

Sophie opened her book at John 3:16

For God so loved the world, that he gave his only begotten Son, that whosoever believeth in him should not perish, but have everlasting life.

Sophie repeated this again and again, and it gradually found its way towards Emma's hearing and then into her understanding.

For God so loved the world, that he gave his only begotten Son, that whosoever believeth in him should not perish, but have everlasting life.

Again and again and again Sophie repeated it, and soon a knot of patients had gathered around, and they were all reciting some of the most powerful words of divine love in scripture. For those who had never heard it, it was easy to learn with two or three repetitions.

In the midst of that place, to where diseased bodies and even diseased souls had been sent, where desolation reigned in the hearts of most, where rejection was their lot and loneliness their fate, where no hope blossomed, no joy bubbled, where tears and cries of despair and pain were daily heard, into that deep leprous cave came Jesus, the Light of the world, on that Christmas Day. Now tears were being copiously shed, tears born of grace, for He gave His love to the rejected, to sinners, to the sick, and to the hopeless. Nell, the 15-year-old who could not remember innocence or happiness, mulled the words over. There was something precious there, like a pearl. Sophie herself was overcome; she missed her dear children today of all days. Sorrow engulfed her but she knew she was not alone in sorrowing. She struggled with forgiving her husband. The others were affected in different ways. Only God knew where they needed to be touched and healed. All felt His presence, loving, powerful, and forgiving.

Emma was no exception. Peace came over her. Her breathing became more regular. Soon, she murmured the powerful truth also. She was half-awake, half-dreaming, a door swung open in her soul. It was a door she had not known was there, and it led to a sweet garden full of gentle colour. It belonged to God, and she was invited to enter.

Someone began to sing *'See Amid the Winter's Snow'*. Someone had a lovely voice. Emma listened. She knew she was loved. Loved by Someone greater than anybody in the world, God, who sent His only begotten son. Who was this Son? She had to know Him! She would know Him! She would ask for forgiveness for her selfishness, and envy, for what had the pursuit of wealth done for her?

Moved to tears, Mrs. Tupper saw a shaft of sunlight come into the ward and embrace the gathering of patients around Emma's bed. She, too, experienced the presence of a loving, patient, and endlessly forgiving God. To the end of her days, she would relate this to anybody who would listen.

A sweet peace descended on the foul ward for the rest of that day.

PATRICK'S CROSS

Patrick tried to put his personal sorrow behind him. He took refuge in prayer, and he formed the habit of paying a visit to a church daily on his way home from the foundry. It was always quiet except when the organist was practising, and usually empty except for a few old women praying their Rosary. There was a comforting presence there, and over several months of frequent visits the Presence made imprints on his soul. He contemplated the images of Jesus carrying His cross, and he knew that He had been there before him, for everybody who would carry one in the future could find comfort that God Himself had borne with sorrow, rejection, and even betrayal.

He could not find it in his heart to blame Emma. He it was who had told her of that first Christmas that she had been found in London. Of course she latched onto the fact that the Leigh-Donners must be her family! Her desperation to belong; her detestation of drudgery as her lot when she felt she was higher! But her blind desire for wealth, that was a false, dangerous god. She'd run after it and intended to marry for money. What he, Patrick, had to offer her, had not been enough. He had a nagging feeling that it would not contribute to her happiness but rather to great misery someday. He took no pleasure in the thought, but rather he feared it.

As for Dudley Pond, if he had done the right thing by Emma and married her, he could make peace with him in his heart. But if he had left her in the dust, that would be hard to forgive and forget. But Patrick did not know, and a part of him did not want to know. Since Mrs. Bowles had left the Carmichaels, there was no further connection with that house, and his sister Lucy had gone into service elsewhere.

He worked long hours at the foundry. One day in early autumn his lifelong friend, Joe 'Whistler' Corbett, sought him out. Whistler's family were tailors and lived not far from the Moores. He was grinning from ear to ear as he approached Pat after he was walking home from the foundry, his hands in his pockets.

"Pat Moore, me old China!"

"You're looking very 'appy today, Whistler; share the news!"

"No news, but I've an idea! I've a mind to go to the Mechanics Institute. Will you enroll wiv me?"

The Mechanics Institute had been founded years before by philanthropist Londoners to provide education for working men.

"Come on, Pat, it will do you good. We get lectures on new inventions, science, and such like. You and I 'ad to leave school at fourteen, which was too early. I want to know more about the world. This age we have now is the best we've ever 'ad! New inventions every day! Will you come? It'll be a lark. We'll improve ourselves no end, and be very knowledgeable in the pub and explaining the world around the dinner table at home, for my Ma and Pa don't understand nothing. I was trying to explain as 'ow a telephone works. Ma said I was 'aving her on and laughed at me."

Whistler had an ulterior motive for getting Patrick to accompany him; his friend needed distraction.

"All work and no play makes Jack a dull boy," he warned him. "Paul Purcell is in too. He's mad for photography. And John Grace wants to get in on all this electricity business, did you see? They're putting electric street lights up now and taking down gas!"

"Will the lamplighters lose their jobs?"

"Perhaps, but that's progress, innit? Come on, Pat, be a sport. Oh oh! Look over there!"

A man on a penny-farthing bicycle wobbled, and he and his bicycle fell to the ground. He was not hurt, but got himself up, embarrassed, righted his bike, dusted off his clothes and mounted it again. A group of children playing had stopped to watch and took off after him, laughing, so that he barely stayed ahead of them, wobbling dangerously as he went.

"Some inventions need improvement," Patrick observed. "I think I might enjoy that institute, if they discuss these kinds of matters."

The subscription was very reasonable, and they thoroughly enjoyed themselves, for it was not like school. There were no exams or tests, and they could attend lectures or read books in the library, or watch experiments in the laboratory, carried out by masters from local schools and colleges, many on a voluntary basis.

The only snag was that he had to leave the foundry a little early on Thursdays to attend, and while the foreman agreed if he should make up the time another day of the week, the owner of the Foundry, Mr. Hodges was not pleased. He was newly rich and showed his status by keeping others down, a mean-mindedness that did not endear him to his employees. Yet, he paid well to keep good men on, and Patrick, like his father and older brother, was a good, solid worker.

"I don't agree with all these institutes," he complained to the foreman. "Moore will get too big for his britches, comin' in here and swaggering, with all the knowledge gained from these lectures."

"But Mr. Hodges, sir, you bettered yourself."

"I did that, Smithers, but not by attending institutes! By hard work!" Smithers knew but did not refer to the fact that his director had inherited the foundry from his great-uncle, in hopes of doing something for the young lad. What his life had been before that, nobody knew, except that he had been very poor.

The young Henry Hodges had run away from a cruel stepfather, had been an urchin for a time, and became involved with a gang of river thieves. By the time the inheritance had come his way, he had found it impossible to extract himself from the gang, who had seen opportunities in having a respectable member as cover. He had married, and his wife had become used to a very good lifestyle.

"I suppose I will have to let him go early," he said grudgingly, but remembering too that he had been given a chance.

Every Thursday evening, Pat and his friends entered the building at Holborn and listened to lectures from explorers, scientists, doctors, and other experts who were happy to impart their knowledge. What with his faith and his new hobby, he was healing from the great wound of losing Emma. He had not courted any other girl, and his friends plotted on how to put some nice girls his way, but they found that Patrick was in no hurry to replace his love.

TWO YEARS LATER

"You're cured." The words were music to Emma's ears. She still suffered from the side effects of the mercury, but not severely.

"Where will you go?" Mrs. Tupper asked her.

"I 'ave nowhere to go," she admitted.

"A lot of folks get jobs here, like me for instance. I was destitute once. I came to Hammersmith from the East End and fell on 'ard times. So I started as an inmate and decided to stay as I was so afeard of livin' on the streets again. Me mother lives in the East End but she can keep 'erself. I don't like 'er way of life, selling fish. If you want to stay, apply to the matron. I've taken a liking to you, Emma, and if you want to work 'ere I'll put in a good word for you."

"That's good of you," Emma said. She might as well work here as anywhere in the workhouse. At least here she could be useful; she'd been through the horrid treatment and understood what the patients endured.

She was growing in faith, had joined a church, and now understood the verses hung at various places around the workhouse buildings. She was free to go where she pleased, and in her off-duty left the sombre buildings to walk to the church where she prayed.

Sophie was cured. She and her husband, also cured and very contrite, were reunited with their children and were slowly getting back on their feet. Jenny was not so lucky; her kidneys failed from the mercury treatment. Poor Jenny was buried in the paupers' graveyard. Nell, the young prostitute, had been taken into a woman's shelter, where she received skills as a seamstress. She never saw her family again, for it was they who had brought about her ruin at a young age. Lily, who had contracted the disease on her honeymoon, was cured also and left. She did not know what became of Lily but remembered her in her prayers.

Knowing these women had done Emma a power of good. They had enlarged her heart and given her a deeper and more compassionate understanding of people.

Emma's application to be a matron was accepted, and she worked there for two years. She was a blessing to the poor women, who had been as wretched as she had been once.

Her way of living now was to be a disciple of Jesus, and that meant a great deal had to be altered. No more envy. It was still possible, when she was out and about, to experience a stab of this desire when she saw a lady in furs and jewellery, but she only had to remind herself that envy was unhealthy for her soul and mind, and she could never be happy if she were envious.

One day, Mrs. Tupper had the information that there was a gentleman fallen on hard times on the male foul ward. He was not likely to live, as he had sought no treatment until very late.

"What's his name?" Emma asked immediately.

"He's a Mr. Pond."

Was it her old lover?

At first, she was angry, then smug, then angry again.

I 'ave to pray for him, she thought. *God expects no less of me! Why has he ended up here? Would his family not have sent him to a private hospital?* She had so many questions, and they nagged her so much, that she went to the men's side and soon found him.

"Well, hallo." Dudley said. "You here too?"

"Yes, and thank you for the gift. I'm cured though. Did you know you 'ad a venereal disease?"

"No, I didn't. Sorry."

She sat on the side of the bed. The handsome face was pocked and haggard, and his lips cracked and dry. His nightshirt hung in huge folds. His wrists were narrower than hers, his neck had deep hollows. He was very ill.

"Why are you in 'ere? Why are you not in a private 'ospital?"

"I couldn't tell my mother and father. I just disappeared. I was found by the police in Regents Park, as ill as you see me now."

"How is your friend Mortimer?"

"I haven't seen him for years. None of my friends kept in contact with me when I got ill. They vanished. I slept on park benches and ate from rubbish bins."

"Did you drug me that day?"

He made no reply.

"You did, didn't you?"

"Who told you?"

"I suspected it, and Mrs. Howard found the vial."

She could tell that he did not have long to live. She felt sorry for him now. His life had been wasted.

"For God so loved the world, that he gave his only begotten Son, that whosoever believeth in him should not perish, but have everlasting life." The words came from her a little reluctantly, for she still harboured some resentment, and

she found she was rather unwilling to share 'the pearl of great price' with him. But she had to because God loved him, too.

"I know the Bible," he said quietly. "I'm going to die soon. I wish I had done better with my life. Is it too late to repent?"

"It's never too late."

"Then I repent. I'm sorry I hurt you. Ruined your life. I have a lot of other sins. God have mercy on me."

He became very pale then, reached for a basin, and vomited a quantity of bright red blood. "I'm sorry," he gasped. Emma did not know if he was apologizing again for using her or for being sick in front of her. She held the basin for him, for he became too weak and almost dropped it. She said nothing, but her quiet silence said everything, and he sank back upon the pillow, his eyes open and glassy, fixed upon the ceiling. The colour drained quickly from his face, and he became very still.

"Dudley?" But he was gone.

"God have mercy on your soul!" she whispered, and found that she meant it.

MY FATHER IS...

It was only a short time later that Mrs. Tupper went on holiday to her mother's for a week. On the Tuesday of that week, Emma was rubbing ointment on a patient and Nurse Archer came in. She was the only trained nurse in the foul wards.

"There's a man to see you," she said. "I'll take over from you. Off you go. I've let him inside, he's in the corridor, but don't be long."

A man! Who could that be? Patrick, perhaps? Oh please, let it be Patrick! I'll tell him how I've changed! How stupid I was! How I loved him, and how I have been thinking of him every day and praying for him too! But no. I can never marry Patrick now!

"It's your father," the nurse added, seeing her astonishment.

Her heart lurched in her chest. Her father! Her father at last! Could it be? After all this time?

"Did he give his name?"

This wasn't as strange a question as might be thought in the workhouse.

"No, he just said he wanted to see Miss Emma Leigh-Donner and that's you, isn't it? And to tell you that it's your father. Lift up your arm a bit more, Mrs. Spalding."

As Emma shut the door behind her, she stopped and took a deep breath to calm the hammering of her heart. In the dim light of the hallway, she saw a man at the other end of it. He was in shadow.

Who was he? Captain Cyril Leigh-Donner, at last? Possibilities swam about in her head. He would be astounded and annoyed that she was here, in Brickhill Workhouse, an attendant in the foul ward, of all places! Would she have to own up to her own history? Surely not.

She had to smile at the prospect of her relatives at Belgravia penitent and embarrassed when she marched in on his arm! She'd take her rightful place among her family. She would be wealthy after all.

But was it Jim Enright after all? Perhaps the couple who looked after her were really her flesh and blood!

She began to walk toward him, and as she did, she observed that he was short and burly, and did not carry a cane, and was not dressed like a gentleman. His dress was that of a working man, and his clothes were baggy.

"My Olga!" He ran to her and doffed his hat, and she saw a shock of coarse white hair in a scraggly, uneven cut. His eyes were an intense blue, his beard and moustache white and scraggly also, and he threw his arms out to embrace her.

"Olga? But who are you?" she cried out.

"I'm your father, Olga, your Papa!"

"But wot's your bloomin' name?" she cried out in a loud voice.

"Richard Brown! Ah, let me look at you - you are the image of my lovely Oksana!" He enclosed her in a bear hug then, as she digested the information, long sought, as to who her father was. She knew now.

Richard 'Dick' Brown, the corporal from Spitalfields.

THE RELATIONS

The next thing her father said was to entreat her to give up her job immediately and come home with him.

"I can't do that, er-Father." The address sounded so strange, but at least she had somebody to call by that address at last.

But Richard Brown! She felt more disappointed than she cared to acknowledge to herself. He was an untidy, vulgar man, built like a barrel. Under his jacket he wore a belted grey tunic, not a proper shirt. His hat was old and battered. He smelled of oil, tobacco, and unwashed clothing. He looked like a man with little or no means.

"How did you find me?"

"My sister's the attendant here, in't she! Betty Tucker! When I heard her say the name Emma Leigh-Donner, I knew it must be you. If you won't come with me now, come this evening when you get off work. You 'ave a day off tomorrow; Betty told me. Come and stay the night. I'll wait for you at the gate at eight fifteen."

Mrs. Tucker was her aunt! She remembered one day when they had been working together side by side, and a sudden noise had startled them, so that they had both looked up and toward it together. A patient who had seen them had said, "Are you two related? You looked so alike there as you turned yer 'eads." They had laughed it off, for neither wished to be likened to the other.

Emma hurried through her work day and rushed to collect a few things from her locker at the end of her shift. He was at the gate, waiting. She was still feeling that all of this was unreal, and she was a little afraid that she'd be swept up into a life that was not appealing to her, but to get to know her father and his family - her family! - she must.

"You must tell me about my mother!" That was her first concern as they set off in the direction of Spitalfields by tube and on foot.

"Ah, she was beautiful! A farmer's daughter, rosy and plump-cheeked. Her dimples! We got married, and you were born in wedlock, my dear, in case you ever wondered about that. But my plans for you did not go right; I can see that now."

"Is my mother alive or dead?"

"Dead eighteen years! That's why I sent you back! I thought, I shall send my daughter back to a good life. Nobody would be any the wiser. But the captain's family did not go for it; still, it was worth a try. I wasn't certain about the lady's Christian name, but I gave it a shot, cos I was footman there, wasn't I? I must've 'eard it said. I was right, wasn't I? The nurse was supposed to take you to the 'ouse but I suppose she 'adn't the nerve. And you kept their surname, 'owever you managed it," he said to her, slyly pleased.

"When did you come back to England?"

"Only the other day. I 'ave to keep my head down." He pulled his hat over his eyes. He talked of the voyage, the food on board, the boring characters he was forced to keep company with, and Emma could not get any more of him about long-ago events.

"There's time for all that," her father said.

"There's so much to talk of!" she exclaimed as they reached the house, the very same crooked house in the squashed-looking street that she had been brought to before, only it seemed to have sagged even more. Her father had pulled his bowler down over his face, almost covering his eyes.

"Is your mother still alive?" Emma clearly remembered the frightening incident in the house when she was a child. But Emma had since learned what to be afraid of, and batty old women were not on her list.

"That she is, she'll go on forever! Dear Ma. Over the moon to see me. Betty is 'ere too." He threw open the decrepit door.

"Me daughter is 'ere!"

The same dark room was even smaller than she remembered; the little fire, and shadowy figures about, one of them more crooked and bent almost over, seated by the fire, and one familiar to her, and a few more who had come to see the long-lost daughter of the house.

Betty was beaming. "You're my niece!" she sang out. "It's no wonder we got on so well. You're my brother's child! Look, Ma! It's Emma!"

"I knew she was ours, but those selfish Enrights kep' her!" shouted the old woman. "I'd a-reared her proper and taught 'er 'as how to sell fish, and she wouldn't 'ave to spend 'er days in the workus. It's bad enough to 'ave you there, the shame of it, but you won't sell fish for anyone."

Emma was invited to sit down on a wobbly three-legged stool and looked at the faces about her.

My relations, she thought. *Can it be true?*

WHAT HAPPENED ON THE HILL

Soon, a cup of water was offered to her, and then Betty disappeared into the kitchen behind them, and she smelled potatoes and fish cooking. The meal was sparse, but an improvement of workhouse fare, for though she was a pauper attendant, her food was little better than the inmates. A cup of watery milk with black specks was provided for her and her alone. They were poor indeed!

The conversation was rich, however, and she hung onto every word of her father's. She was all ears to hear what had happened that fateful day with Captain Leigh-Donner and Corporal Enright.

"We 'ad just reached a copse of bushes, and next thing bullets were flying over our 'eads, and I says to the captain, get down or you'll get it, and I raised my 'and to pull 'im down but it was too late, he got 'it in the back.

Enright 'ad got it straightaway. I rolled off into some shrubbery and hid there. But they moved off somewhere else, down the hill I was sure, and I 'eard a lot of firin' and explosions. At night, I started to make my way down the other side of the hill toward a farm. I'd seen it earlier. It was an enemy farm right enough, but I took my chances."

"Why didn't you go back down to your own side, Father?"

"Because I'd fall straight into the 'ands of the enemy." Her father rushed on with his story, not liking the interruption. "Now I crept toward it and soon was in a barn. In the barn was a sick cow lyin' down, an' I got a sack an' put it over its back, like I 'eard is done in Lancashire, from a fellow I knew from there, and the cow stood up. The farmer 'eard something, and I put my 'ands up and gave myself up. Well 'is name was Pyotor Chakalov."

It was a disjointed and somewhat fantastic story. The farmer did not agree with the war, did not like the Tsar, and after he saw the cow upon her feet, he brought the frozen, hungry man into his own house, and his granddaughter, a lovely lass of sixteen or so, gave the young corporal warm milk and bread. Pyotor lived in an isolated place, had the rheumatics bad, and Dick, of his own accord, found a hammer and nails and began to patch things up around the house the following day, with Oksana showing him where the repairs needed to be done. It snowed hard, and even if he had tried to get back to his lines, it would have been impossible.

After the snow melted, he made the decision to stay with Pyotor and his granddaughter Oksana. It was a cosy, happy home, and he was needed there, and he was falling in love. After some time, English soldiers came to the farm, and he hid in a little space under the roof until they'd gone. Pyotor denied any knowledge of the party of three that the men were searching for.

"And they never found the bodies. That's what I 'eard," Betty said. "That's why they never knew whose child *she* was!"

Her father shifted in his chair.

"Why din't they find the bodies, Dick?" Betty asked.

"Are you all stupid!" Emma's grandmother snorted. "If they'da found two, they'd knowed who was missin' and they'd 'ave gone arter Dick! You took 'em away, did you, son?"

"Mother, not so loud!" Her son spoke in hushed tones. "The walls 'ave ears! Yes, I went up and buried 'em as soon as the snow melted."

"You're a clever lad, orright," said his mother proudly. "An' I bet you stripped 'em too, fer if they'd a been dug up arter, they'd a known who was missin' by their stripes an' what they carried in their pockets. Did you get anyfink good off the captain?"

"Mother!" Betty hushed her. Emma's father ignored the question. Emma found herself deflated by hearing of her father's actions. She was as patriotic as any English person. Desertion she could understand, the cosy warmth of a farmhouse instead of a freezing hillside, and falling in love to boot, but to have robbed the dead captain? She did not want to think of that.

"Father," she asked him eagerly, changing the subject to one closer to her heart. "Do you have any likeness of my mother?"

He seemed happy the subject had changed, and he went to the corner where he slept, and took something from his jacket which was hanging up on a hook.

"There she is. Isn't she beautiful?"

Emma held in her hands the first likeness of her mother that she had ever seen. She took it under the light and peered at it as closely as she could. She was dressed in a style of costume Emma was unfamiliar with, and a scarf was around most of her head. Her fair hair had a middle parting, her eyes were soft and expressive, a little smile played about her lips, and she had dimples. She looked light-hearted and kind. Emma pressed it to her heart and burst into sobs.

"There, there," said her father, coming to her and putting his hand on her head. "She was luverly, wasn't she? Would anybody blame me for leaving the army for Oksana Chaklova? The only woman I ever loved. How she doted on you! Then she took ill with a fever, and we lost her. I didn't feel up to raising a girl, so I gave you to a

Nightingale nurse who had stayed on after the war and was coming 'ome for good. It's a pity you din't get the good education, the finery, and the prospects that I planned for you, but I tried. You've turned out good though, fer all that."

Emma felt a little amused in her grief, that her father thought she'd 'turned out good' when she'd spent the last several years in the workhouse. These people were easy to please!

EMMA AND HER FATHER

Three wooden planks were laid side by side to connect two chairs, and a straw mattress covered in ticking was laid upon it, and two blankets borrowed from next-door, and that was the bed shared by Emma and her aunt Betty. Even if it had been comfortable, Emma would not have slept well with this new turn in her life.

The following morning, after a breakfast of thin porridge and tea, which was still better than the workhouse, Emma and her father decided to go for a walk. He wanted to see where she grew up, but Emma did not want to go back to Whitechapel.

He was vexed, and he pressed her for the reason. She had to admit to him that she did not want to meet one of her neighbours, a young man named Patrick Moore.

"Is it he gave you that- that-?" her father asked belligerently.

Emma was mortified that Betty had told him about the disease.

"I know about it, and I intend to do something about it too. I'm your father!"

"Er, no - that wasn't Patrick, it was a gentleman - I was drugged one day and -"

"Where is 'e?" her father looked thunderous. "He'll be brown bread by the time I've finished with him!"

"He's dead. He died of it."

"Good. I'm saved the trouble."

"Father, am I baptized?" Emma changed the subject.

"Yes, of course you are, dipped three times in the water."

Then Emma wished to know everything about her mother that her father could tell her, and she drank in all the information that she could.

"I want you to finish up in the workus," he said to her, and it felt like a command. "I want to provide for you. We'll make a 'ome together, you and me."

"Where? At your mother's?"

"No, it's too small. We'll move to another 'ouse, the three of us, if we can persuade Mother. I 'ave money. I sold a gold watch I found lying about the ship. I got twenty-five pounds for it."

Emma wondered about the 'lying about' part, but she did not ask any questions. She considered the proposition.

"I don't know," she said.

"What do you mean? I'll work, and while I'm working you care for Ma and do the 'ousekeeping. Let Betty continue on as she wishes. She wouldn't know how to live anywhere else except Brick'ill."

"I'm to go back there tomorrow. I'll think about it."

"You can 'ave a room to yourself, with a fire."

A room of her own, just as when she was growing up! How nice it would be not to have to live in a dormitory which, in spite of forty or more people sleeping there, was cold nine months of the year!

"All right then, Father."

A house was rented which had two rooms upstairs and two downstairs. Emma and her father slept in the rooms upstairs; the Grandmother had a cosy little alcove by the fire, ensuring her warmth in winter. Dick got work doing odd jobs, though it became more and more sporadic, so that he hardly left the house after a few months, claiming that he'd met a fellow he had known long ago who recognised him and it would be better not to go out so much. Grandmother took Emma every day to the fish market to teach her the trade, and after a few months Emma found that it was she and her old grandmother who were the breadwinners, and it was hard work indeed, but she was used to hard work.

Then Grandmother Brown got a bad cold, and then pneumonia. She lay on her alcove couch and coughed the nights away. Emma looked after her as best she could until she finally had no strength to cough anymore, her lungs filled with fluid, and she breathed her last.

It was then Emma and her father, and Emma was the sole earner, cook, and housekeeper when she returned after a long chilly day at Spitalfield Markets, for her father expected to be waited on hand and foot.

THE NEW WORLD

Emma spent much of her time at the market shouting herself hoarse selling eels, haddock, skate, and cod. The days were long, and the weather was usually cold. Sometimes she felt ill, and this was to be expected, for the mercury had long-term effects upon her body and its systems.

In summertime, the smells were strong and though she was used to bad smells, sometimes she wished she could be away from the city and begin her life all over again. She always had her eyes peeled for someone she knew from Whitechapel, and one day she saw, in the distance, a familiar male figure who was walking with a young woman. She kept her eyes on him while wrapping a fish in newspaper for a customer, taking money, and giving change. The figure neared; now she was sure! It was Patrick Moore with a girl on his arm. They were coming her way! She ducked behind her stall until they had passed by and missed a few customers, but she did not wish to be seen.

Patrick had gone on with his life. He had a new sweetheart. Perhaps this girl was even his wife! It would be very difficult if he came along again with the girl. He could come to her and say, *"Emma, meet my wife, Mrs. Moore."*

Her heart became heavy with the prospect that one day, he would find another girl, settle down, and have a family. She often became morose and tense in the market, for if they had come this way once, might they not come a second time?

She was in this mood one day when her father said, "I don't like to live in England anymore. There's nothing 'ere for me, girl."

"But Father-!" Emma was upset. Though she and her father had arguments, she did not want him to go away. She would feel abandoned.

"What is it, child? You don't want me to go away, do you?"

"No, I don't."

"Then come with me! We'll get a new start, you and me, in America."

"America! Father, that's so far away!"

"Not at all. We wouldn't bide in New York though, or any city, for in Russia I got a taste for the country life, healthy, open, and airy. We'd go west. We'd lay claim to a piece of land and 'ave a little farm, but not too far away from civilisation either, for you will 'ave to get a husband."

"Oh." Emma thought her chances of marriage were greatly reduced.

"In the west, men outnumber women. Any woman who goes there is beset by all the bachelors in town as soon as she alights the train. She can be married by sunset if she 'as a mind to."

Emma considered this. Perhaps she could marry. A widower perhaps. A widower could have a family already, and might not mind not having any from his second wife. She could be an instant mother to several children!

"Will we go, Emma?"

"All right, Father, we'll go!"

"The sooner the better then." He lifted a pair of gold cufflinks out of his pocket and jiggled them in his hand. "This will see us to America."

"Father, where did you get those?

"They fell off a cart," he chuckled.

"People are very careless with their cuff links," Emma said in cross voice. She was not at all happy about her father's sticky fingers and more than once had remonstrated with him, to no avail.

In America, it would be different. A fresh beginning, a new life!

THE FOUNT

Patrick had learned a great deal at the institute, and he found much of it useful for his work. He was particularly interested in the books about Technical Drawing and Typesetting, and when he had spare time, he began to design his own fount at home. The alphabet in uppercase and lowercase, bold and italics, narrow and wide, and his mother sighed sometimes as she waited for the kitchen table late at night so that she could set out the supper. But she was impressed. His father was enthusiastic.

"A little more ornament would set it apart, a little upward curl perhaps."

His father had an instinct for good design and was a great adviser. "I think a little shading on the uppercase would set it off, you know, for 'eadlines."

"Father, you and I can go into business together, perhaps!"

"You have to have capital for that. What will you call it, Moore's Type?"

"Too plain, Father! Moore Ornamental, perhaps."

"Moore Ornamental Serif?"

"Is there any need to say Serif, if you say Ornamental?"

They discussed back and forth; his mother thought that a fancier variation for invitation cards should be designed also, and Patrick listened to all, accepting and rejecting, and there were weeks of enthusiastic discussions, until they were all satisfied that Moore Ornamental was as fine as it could be.

It soon got to Mr. Hodges' ears that Patrick was designing a typeface, and he expressed interest.

"Perhaps we will manufacture and promote it to our buyers," he said with enthusiasm. "Will you show me the designs? We can have a specimen sheet made up and show it to our clients!"

Patrick was excited at the thought and brought in his rolls of paper, and showed him the fount drawn in sharp pencil, encased in meticulously ruled lines with precise measurements, and notes he made in the margins.

"It's very impressive, Moore," said Mr. Hodges, after examining them. "Very good indeed. May I hold on to this for a few days?"

Patrick was reluctant, but he agreed. What harm could it do?

The few days went by, and the designs were not returned to him. He approached Mr. Hodges.

"Oh, Moore, I ought to have told you. I brought them home to show to my wife. She has flair for this sort of thing and is interested in seeing them."

"With respect, Mr. Hodges, I did not think you would remove the drawings from this building!"

"Oh, if I had realised you were that way about it, I would not have done so, but my wife is so interested! I shall have them for you tomorrow! It will be a few months before I can give you a decision about them."

But it was three days later, after another request, before they were handed back. The excuse was that Marge's mother had arrived unexpectedly, throwing the Hodges' household into confusion. "Fortunate you are that you do not have a mother-in-law, Patrick," Mr. Hodges said with a wink, trying to appease him, for Patrick was stony faced as he rolled up the sheets of paper, having ascertained that they were all present.

Several weeks went by, and one day Patrick asked Mr. Hodges if he had considered manufacturing the new fount.

"Moore, I have brought it to the board, but the decision is that it is quite difficult to get printers and publishers to accept new founts. There's the Daily Reader, using the same old typeface for many years, and others that do not want to alter anything, though a fresh look would bring new life to some of those old publications. I do not wish to go to the trouble and expense of producing a new type only to incur a loss when nobody goes for it."

Patrick had to acknowledge the truth of this, and realised that it may be up to him to get magazines, newspapers, and printers interested in the new Moore Ornamental, and if Hodges was not going to manufacture it, he may have to look into borrowing money for another foundry to make the metal type. It seemed like an expensive, gargantuan task, however, and very risky financially. He was not sure where to begin and was about to do some more research into the matter at the institute when he learned something very suspicious.

Mr. Hodges had, for some time, been casting a new fount he was calling Sweet Margaret. Kelly and White were sworn to discretion as they worked on it. But somehow, the word got about, and Patrick insisted on inspecting the sheets. Kelly reluctantly produced the specimen sheets, and Patrick saw instantly that it was his own.

Mr. Hodges had stolen his design! He had copied it in the days it had been at his home.

"Mr. Hodges," he began as soon as he went to work the following morning, for he never did anything impulsively and wanted to think about the matter overnight, "there is a serious matter I wish to discuss with you."

Hodges did not look at him, but pretended to be very busy with some papers. "Hurry up, Moore, I have a directors meeting soon."

"That new Sweet Margaret fount is my fount."

"It most certainly is not your fount."

"Yes, it is, in every respect! I have examined it! It is exactly the same, right down to the ornaments and measurements! You 'ave stolen my design!"

Hodges must have been expecting this accusation, for he rose to his feet and shouted, "Your fount was designed and drawn up on work time in those times when I was not here; therefore it belongs to me."

"I beg to differ, Mr. Hodges. I never used work time."

"Of course you did. The paper itself is our drawing paper!"

"It is similar, but not yours; I purchased it myself. You're accusin' me of stealing paper, while you stole my design! And I never used work time; it was all done at 'ome in my own time. You may ask the other employees."

"I have. Kelly and White affirmed that they saw you take out paper and use it when I was not here."

Kelly and White. Two sycophants on their way up. Thick as thieves!

"I won't stand for this, Mr. Hodges. Theft is serious."

Patrick's father was in the office now, having been alerted to the shouts coming from there.

"You are discharged immediately from this foundry!" Mr. Hodges shouted to Patrick.

"You're bein' a bit 'ard, Mr. Hodges," Mr. Moore objected.

"Do you want the door too?" the director fired back.

Patrick motioned his father to be silent. There was no point in putting all the menfolk of the Moore household out of work.

"I intend to take this further," were Patrick's last words to his boss as he collected his wages and left.

PATRICK RETURNS

Patrick was so angry that he went straight to the police and made a formal complaint. The desk sergeant took down the details but did not seem to think there was anything he could do about the matter, and that Patrick would be better off engaging an attorney to take his case to court.

Patrick knew little of the law, but in thinking about the matter, he walked back to the foundry in order to meet Mr. Percy there. He was in charge of supplies. If Patrick had stolen a roll of paper, Percy would know of it. When he got there, however, he waited for him to come out, but he did not come; perhaps he had gone home early. He had come back for nothing.

A few of his old workmates saw him and stopped to sympathise with him on his hard luck with Hodges. Kelly and White slunk by, pretending not to see him.

The light was on in Mr. Hodges' office, and he debated going up to ask him to come to a reasonable solution for both of them but decided that was a waste of time also. As he turned from the gate, he saw two men go around the back of the building. He recognised one as being a man who often visited Mr. Hodges in his office. When he did so, the door was always shut for privacy, but occasionally arguments could be heard there. The gossip was that the man worked for him in his other business, which nobody seemed to know much about. It was nothing to do with the production of metal type, that much was certain.

Patrick went home. His mother had supper ready, and they sat down to eat.

"Where's Ollie?" Pat looked around for his younger brother, a man as tall as him and who looked very like him.

"He's gone to Fulham. There's a football match there. That lad is football mad," his mother said. "But Patrick, what are you to do now?"

"I don't know, Ma. I'll think of something."

"Becky won't be happy when she hears of this. Her father is very strict about her keeping company with a man who has work."

He and Becky were going steady.

NEW WORLD

Three days to go before leaving for America! Emma was by turns grieved and excited. Grieved because she would leave Patrick and the Moore family behind her forever. She found herself not wishing to leave without saying goodbye to them.

But it was a new beginning. She was still young; perhaps she could put everything behind her, firmly into the past, and start again in that growing country of opportunity, America.

"Tickets," her father said, pleased, laying two little blue cards upon the table. "The *Saxonia* packet steamer, leaving on the first tide on Wednesday next, calling to Southampton to pick up passengers, then Queenstown for the Irish, and arriving in New York the following Monday. I spoke to a packet rat, and he says it's the fastest passage."

"What shall we do when we get to New York? Where will we stay?"

"I don't know that yet, girl, but we won't stay there very long! We'll head west as soon as we can. We might even get on one of those wagon trains to take us there. Now that'd be an adventure! You'll be married before you know it."

"I don't know that, Father. You know I can't 'ave children."

"Don't tell your any of your suitors that if he likes you and 'as money!"

"What kind of man would you like to see me married to, Father?"

"Any man who will keep me in beer."

"Oh, Father, be serious!"

Her father could be exasperating and amusing by turns, and though they quarelled often, for they had strong opinions, they were becoming good friends. Gone was the regret that she was not from Belgravia. She knew better than to grieve for people to whom she had meant nothing, or for the trappings of their lives.

But Patrick! Would she ever cease to think of him? The memory of him arm-in-arm with the girl haunted her. He would of course get on with his life and be happy with another. Did he ever think of her?

"You never noticed we 'ave second class accommodations," her father said. "I'm to share with another mister, and I assume a miss will share with you. It's going to be very comfortable indeed, for the food is vastly superior to steerage."

"Father, how could you afford -?" He chuckled and turned away. Emma did not like this dishonesty.

"Father, you must promise me not to steal anyfink before we go," she implored him. "I have 'eard as to the police in England can telegraph the police in America, and a thief can be apprehended by the American police and sent back to England to face justice!"

"Is that true?" Her father sounded like a child who was about to be deprived of a special treat. "They're getting too smart for their boots. Wot is the world comin' to?"

"And please don't nick anyfink from your cabin mate. And another thing, America may not 'ave justice as we have, and you could be in the nick if they think you're dodgy. And they all 'ave guns! Be 'onest, Father!"

"It seems as if you're dead set ter keep me on the straight a' narrow, Miss. I don't like being told what ter do, so keep your trap shut, or I'll marry you off to the first man I meet in New York and set off for the west on my ownsome. What's for supper? I'm 'ungry."

"I hadn't time to get anytink ready. Bread and cheese will 'ave to do."

"Bread an' cheese an' beer. This time next week, we'll be sittin' down to hot mutton stew, dumplings, and custard puddin'."

"It'll be nice not to 'ave to cook for a few weeks," Emma said. She was quite looking forward to the voyage and the leisure it promised, like a holiday! She could spend all day lying on a deckchair if she pleased, only getting up to be served her meals! She hoped she would have a pleasant cabin companion, and perhaps they'd take walks around the decks and enjoy the fresh air.

She could leave England behind her very well. She could.

"Well, I never!" Her father was reading the newspaper. "What was the name of that bloke your old beau used to work for? The man with the foundry?"

"His name is Hodges. What of him?"

"He's dead, that's what. Murdered. Fished from the Thames at Hammersmith."

HEARTBREAK AGAIN

This news propelled Emma even more to see Patrick, knowing as much as she did about Hodges from when she had lived at Hammersmith. The Moore family would be disturbed by this news and by the uncertainty it would bring them.

"Where are you off to?" her father asked her, seeing her get her bonnet and shawl.

"Never you mind," she replied, and escaped the house before she could get a clip on the ear.

"You'd better be back afore ten!" her father howled after her.

She walked quickly along the streets that led to Whitechapel, stopping only at a sweet shop, remembering that where there were Moores, there were little ones. As familiar landmarks began to come into view, her emotions rose with bittersweet memories of her childhood. She could hear the voices of children playing as she turned into Lilac Lane.

The Lane had not changed much, except that the Enright house had a red door and new curtains. Three children ran about on the street and when they saw her go to the Moore door, they joined her. She smiled at them, and they smiled back. Their eyes were upon the bag of sticky treats in her hand.

The Moore's house looked just the same, and she took a deep breath and knocked on the door. Would they even know her?

Mrs. Moore answered, at first surprised, and if she had any hard feelings toward Emma, she hid them well as she invited her inside, the three little ones in hot pursuit for the sweets.

The kitchen was as she remembered it; warm, inviting, and full. Several familiar faces looked at her, as astonished as Mrs. Moore's. There was quite a crowd there, Lucy with her husband, Mary with hers, and the eldest son Dennis. Children of various ages swarmed everywhere. One of them was sitting on Patrick's lap.

The surprised adults got up from chairs to greet her, swinging infants into their arms from their laps or depositing toddlers upon the floor. Certainly, it was a great surprise, and one thing occurred to all of them. Emma was not married, or at least not to a rich man, for her dress was poor as theirs, perhaps even more so.

Her eyes were upon Patrick's, and his upon hers. There was a mixture of pleasure and reserve in both pairs of eyes. He was glad to see her, but the remembrance of their last meeting had brought a great searing flame to his heart again. And for Emma's part, her pain was that he did not and would never know that she had contracted a shameful disease and had spent two years not just in the workhouse, but in the very worst part of it, and that she was unable to have children.

But Patrick wondered how she had been brought to this impoverished state. He took no pleasure in the fact that obviously her dreams had been dashed. He burned to know as she was offered a chair.

"I wanted to say goodbye before I left," Emma began. "My father and I leave for New York in three days."

"Your father!" they chorused.

"Yes, and I'm sure you will want to know who he is! He is Corporal Richard Brown."

There was a silence. Patrick felt sorry for her and pleased at the same time. Emma was surely cured of her ambition to be of the ton and live at Belgravia if she had accepted her lowly father into her heart. He wondered if it had been very hard.

"He survived the ambush," she said. "He married a Crimean girl, me mother. I saw 'er photograph."

"I'm so 'appy for you, dear!" Mrs. Moore burst out. "I can see that you are more at peace, knowin'! Did your mama pass away, then? Is that why you was sent back? And your father tried to pass you off as the captain's child?"

"Yes, exactly so, Mrs. Moore. He took a chance that they'd keep me and make a fine lady of me!" She laughed easily, and they all laughed with her when they realised that it was all right to do so.

"How did you find 'im?" Patrick found his voice. He was growing more tranquil and more pleased every moment. He'd seen the beloved dimples flash before him. He had also, as had his mother and sisters, seen that no wedding band was to be seen upon her fingers, for she had taken off her gloves.

"He found me." That would do for an answer.

"I heard about Mr. Hodges," she said then. "I wonder - I wonder if I could perhaps speak in private to you, Mr. Moore?"

It took Patrick a moment to realise she was looking at him. He sprang up, handing his little nephew to his mother.

"Of course, Miss er - *Brown*!" He grinned. "Shall we go for a walk?"

As they made their way along, she told him that at one time she had lived at Hammersmith and been party to a very odd conversation, and that her landlady later explained to her what it must have meant.

"Smuggling!" Patrick was astounded.

"I thought to tell you, before I go."

He stopped and faced her.

"You are not married to that Pond man," he said.

"No. He had no intention of marriage."

"So what have you been doing?"

"As I said, I lived at Hammersmith for a time, in service to Mrs. Howard. Sometime after that my father found me, and he and I 'ave been a family since then. He had a mother, the old hag I once told you about, only she was not so bad. She taught me to sell fish, and I sold them at Spitalfields market. And I have an aunt. And some cousins."

"You never married."

"No, and I do not know that I ever will, Patrick."

"Are you determined to go to New York?"

"Yes, quite so," Emma said quietly.

"You could stay," he said.

Emma's heart fluttered in hope, but then she dashed her own hopes, with the shame of the pox, the foul ward, the mercury treatment that left her unwell sometimes and worst of all, *sterile*. What a horrible-sounding word that was, *sterile*! She would have to tell him all that.

"I'm going, Patrick."

Patrick was silent.

"I wish you well, then," he said, holding out his hand formally.

"And I you. I saw you once, you know, in Spitalfields market. You had a girl on your arm. She looked nice."

Patrick made no reply for a moment, but looked into the middle distance, as if not knowing what to say, before he said, "She is nice. She is Miss Shaw."

"Soon to be Mrs. Moore," Emma said.

Patrick made no reply.

"How are you getting back to Spitalfields?"

"As I came, on my pins."

"Not on your own."

"Dear Patrick," she cried out. "You 'avent changed! I wish I 'ad listened to your advice! How I wish I had not gone alone to that 'ouse that day! How my life would have been so different!"

"I did tell you not to go without Mrs. Bowles."

"Mrs. Bowles? What had she to do with anyfink?"

"I wrote you a letter. The Pond geezer, bottom feeder, came to the foundry, asked me not to stand in your way, and told me that Mrs. Bowles was going wiv you."

"He told you a porky! I never got your letter. Oh, Pat, if I 'ad known he'd told you a porky! I would not 'ave gone! I would've known then-!"

In an instant, his arms were about her.

"It's not too late," he whispered into her ear. "Dearest Emma, I told you I would forgive you. Will you stay? Please?"

She wrestled herself from his arms and turned her back. The tears were flowing fast down her cheeks, and she did not wish him to see them.

"No," she said at last. "Go 'ome, Patrick. It's of no use. Please believe me. I'm going to America with my father."

"Why, Emma?"

"Why does anybody go to America? I'm going to seek my fortune!"

When she turned around, he had gone. She sobbed all the way home to Spitalfields. Her father pretended not to hear her sniffles when she came into the house. He guessed where she had been. The sooner she left England the better, and he'd pick out a good man for her.

THE SUFFRAGETTE

The *Saxonia* pulled out from the dockside, and Emma was composed on the deck as she watched London ebb away. They sailed around the coast, bound for Southampton, and then to Queenstown in Ireland, to pick up the last of the passengers for New York.

Her cabin mate was a Miss Weekes, who was a schoolteacher. She was quiet and read a great deal, and Emma thought that she would be a great bore for the voyage. Her father's cabin mate was a man of forty, a bachelor, with a silver watch on a chain, and silver cufflinks. Emma prayed that he would still be in possession of them after he disembarked at New York.

The meeting with Patrick had done her more harm than good. She felt wretched and torn and had cried so much that she felt her heart dried up. She longed to chat with another woman, but Miss Weekes was not interested in chat. The only sentence she addressed to her cabin mate was: "Don't you think women should have the vote?" When Emma said she had never thought about it, Miss Weekes buried herself in her reading again, and when they docked at Southampton, she contrived to get a newspaper for that day.

"Well, what a nerve!" she said to Emma that evening as they were tucked into their beds and the ship was steaming along by the Cornish coast. The light was still on, and Emma wished to put it out, but Miss Weekes had not finished her reading.

"I am outraged beyond telling!" She passed the newspaper across to the other bed. "See there, the article on the bottom left! How dare an M.P. say that the inferior intellects of women will ensure that he will never support the campaign for the vote! Take it, Miss Brown! Read it for yourself!"

Emma took the newspaper, but in an instant another headline caught her eye.

"Cor blimey!" she shrieked.

"I am gratified you feel as you do, Miss Brown! I had thought you were unconcerned! Forgive me."

But Emma was not listening. She craned toward the gas lamp they shared to read the article.

WHITECHAPEL MAN ARRESTED FOR MURDER. Police yesterday arrested Mr. Patrick Moore, of Lilac Lane, Whitechapel, for the murder of his former employer, Mr. Henry Hodges, in Hammersmith last Friday night. It is understood that the accused had been discharged from his work for theft and subsequently followed Mr. Hodges to Hammersmith, where he was stabbed and thrown into the river. A witness came forward to say that a man fitting the description of Mr. Moore was seen in the area.

"I 'ave to get off this ship!" Emma screamed.

"Why? Why?" Miss Weekes jumped up in bed. "We are not going to do violence to him, Miss Brown! Egregious he may be but -"

"Oh, 'ang the MP! Who cares about 'im? My love is accused of murder, and I 'ave to help him, for I know someone who knows someone who might 'ave done it!"

Miss Weekes was all agog, all her own concerns forgotten, and Emma agonised as to how she was going to get away and back to England to save Mr. Moore from the hangman.

QUEENSTOWN

"**G**etting off at Queenstown? No, you're not." Her father was livid. "What 'ave I done to deserve such an ungrateful stubborn child?"

"I am past twenty-one and may do as I please," Emma said tartly. "As soon as Mr. Moore is safe, then I can follow you, can't I?"

"Perhaps, but in steerage. You're missing out on a week of good vittles."

But Emma would not be moved. Miss Weekes, Stephanie, supported her. She should be able to do as she pleased. And when she found out that Emma had hardly two pennies to rub together, she gave her five pounds.

"You may need to bribe the prison wardens," she said. "Another matter, Emma, is that he will need good legal counsel. My cousin, James Weekes, is a barrister at the

Old Bailey. Go and see him, mention my name, and good luck. He will not charge you if you give him this." She produced a gold ring. "It was my grandmother's, and I know he will take it as payment. I am writing a note for you to give to him."

"Why are you doin' this for me?" Emma asked her in astonishment.

"Because I can see you love him, and though I am considered unfairly to be a stone-hearted bluestocking, I'm very tender-hearted and wish I could find a man who will love me. I do not want my grandmother's ring; I want my own..."

"Perhaps in America, Stephanie."

"Everything seems possible in America, Emma! I have another favour to ask. I have a letter for you to put in the post. It's to the editor of the London Times refuting the words of that horribly ignorant member. I have used so many esoteric words that it will send the MP running for a dictionary to understand them."

"Yes, I will post it, I promise." Emma had no idea what esoteric meant, nor did she care.

"Goodbye, dear Father. I'm glad we met again," Emma kissed his cheek on the chilly morning when the *Saxonia* sat offshore in the picturesque Queenstown. He grew misty-eyed.

"Mind you follow someday!" he bellowed, as she descended into the tug. It had deposited several dozen Irish immigrants onto the ship, and it would return to Queenstown with only herself and a few officials of the shipping line and bags of mail. She saw the ship grow smaller and disappear as it steamed its way deeper into the Atlantic ocean, and finally it was gone. She was without a father again.

Back in Whitechapel three days later, she booked into a cheap boarding house. It was late at night. She wrapped herself up in her blanket and slept for a time, for she had not slept on the trains nor the ferry. The ring she kept carefully wrapped in a handkerchief in her reticule.

She found out that he was being held in Newgate Prison, a notorious place known for overcrowding, dirt, and violence.

NEWGATE

She presented herself at the prison and was refused entry; however a half-crown did the trick. Three half-crowns later she was sitting in a cold and draughty room waiting for a warden to bring the prisoner out to her. There were other prisoners there also with visitors, and there was no privacy. The smell of unwashed bodies and clothes pervaded everywhere, for the prisoners were held in cells comprising thirty or forty in number, and washing facilities were very poor.

The door opened, and he shuffled in, for he was in irons. Dressed in dirty clothing, his hair matted, his face unshaven, his eyes widened in astonishment when he beheld his visitor.

"Emma! I thought you were -"

"I was. I disembarked in Ireland and came straight back."

"But, why?"

"Because I saw in a newspaper that you'd been nicked, and I want to 'elp you. I know you didn't do this. Have you got counsel?"

"No. They are expensive. I don't know -"

She told him briefly about Mr. Weekes. "I will get 'im for you. I will explain all later. Patrick." Her voice dropped. "I know someone who knows somethin' about all this. Remember, when I saw you a few weeks ago, I told you that I over'eard a conversation in Hammersmith? I will go back there to find out more."

"No, Emma, no, don't go to that 'ouse again. That's where you went before, wasn't it? It didn't go well then. I know that 'ouse, I was there when I was lookin' for you, I met an evil little gnome called Mortimer."

"If you die, I want to die," she said unexpectedly, banging her fist on the table and tears filling her eyes. He looked at her curiously.

"Then why-"

"I can't say. It's too public 'ere. Pat, I 'ave suffered deeply in my body and in my soul and learned some very 'ard lessons. When you get out, I will tell you, I promise."

The deep emotion and agonized expression that accompanied her statement melted his heart and increased his love for her even more. He had to get out of prison.

"There's something that might be 'elpful, Emma. Tell Mr. Weekes that on the day that Mr. Hodges was murdered, I saw two men go into the building after everybody had left. There was just a light left on in his office. And the other thing is that the witness saw my brother Ollie, not me, in Fulham, which is near to Hammersmith. I have told the police, but the lies of Kelly and White are placing me at the foundry. They said they saw me go in. The police contend that I confronted Hodges there and getting no satisfaction, that I followed 'im to Hammersmith and committed the deed. They found a fancy 'andkerchief with my initials on it, P.M. As if my busy mother or sisters 'ad the time to embroider my initials onto 'andkerchiefs! Emma? *Do not go after evidence.* Do not go down to the Howards. Leave it to the proper channels, to Mr. Weekes. Promise?"

"I can't promise, Pat," she answered at once.

He smiled a little, and there was love in his eyes. Love and hope.

"How did you get in to see me?" he asked then.

"Oh, that reminds me. I 'ave to post a letter," she said, suddenly changing the subject to something that sounded very trivial, which he found quite funny.

"You are a card, Emma Brown."

RIVERSEDGE AGAIN

Emma went straight to Mr. Weekes office, but she found it closed due to the funeral of his partner's father. This was unfortunate. There was a sign saying that it would be open tomorrow, but she did not have the patience to wait. Setting all cautions aside, she ignored Patrick's advice. She would go to Hammersmith herself, now, and visit Mrs. Howard. She caught the underground train there.

She had not seen the house for a long time, and it brought back the memories of the day she had first visited here, that fateful day that had altered her life forever and almost killed her.

The door was answered by a face she recognised, Tilly, grown now, pretty, and healthy, the girl who scavenged for items to stay alive, who Emma had introduced to Mrs. Howard.

The girls were very happy to see each other, but Tilly left her in the hallway to run to Mrs. Howard to tell her who the visitor was. Emma regarded the fateful staircase while she was gone. How different her life might have been had she never ascended that stair!

Mrs. Howard emerged from the back of the house where she sat at nights, but her greeting was cool, and Emma was not asked to come in.

"Are you not going to invite me in, Mrs. Howard?" she said.

"Well, step inside then."

In her warm kitchen, in the presence of Tilly, who was now sewing quietly by the light of a lamp, Emma poured out her story.

"That is all very serious, Emma," she said. "He might well hang. I don't rightly know what you should do, though. Would you like to stay here tonight, and sleep on it? Tomorrow, I might 'ave a good idea."

"Are you sure you don't know some more about the tobacconist shop, Mrs. Howard? What's the name of the man who runs it? He was involved in the smuggling, I'm sure of it!"

"No, Bertie must've been talking of something else, I'm sure," Mrs. Howard said. "I've known Bertie all my life. It wasn't Bertie whom Hodges was talking to that day. It was somebody else."

"But Bertie must know that somebody else," Emma said. "If I stay the night, will you come with me tomorrow morning to ask him?"

"Why, yes, of course. We'll go ask him. I doubt he'll remember though. And I'm not so sure it was that Mr. Hodges you saw, for all that. Maybe somebody like him."

Emma felt deflated after this conversation and changed the subject, asking the old lady if the nice young couple were still in the apartment.

"Er, no, they left a long time ago. Mrs. Ellis imagined all sorts of noises when she was there alone, and they left."

"So who is there now?"

"A single gentleman." Emma was curious about her tone, but she said no more as Mrs. Howard told Tilly to drop her sewing and make up a bed for her visitor in one of the vacant rooms.

There was no key to lock herself in, as was often done if there were male boarders or strangers in the house. What did it matter? She was safe here.

But after Emma lay down, she heard a key turn quietly in the lock. She sat up immediately. What was going on? Why was she being locked in the room? Was it in case a male lodger intruded upon her privacy? When Emma had worked here, it had never been done. Women boarders could lock themselves in if they wished, but never had Mrs. Howard locked any boarder in her room.

She got up, troubled, and struck a match to light the candle. She tried the door, which was locked. This made her agitated. Mrs. Howard knew something and did not want her to find out. Then she heard the front door open and close. Her room was at the back of the house. Someone had gone out, for there were no sounds from downstairs.

THE PURSUER

"Help! Help!" Emma shouted as loud as she could, hoping to awaken the other boarders. She heard murmurs, beds creaking, then doors opening and shutting. At last, the key turned in her lock and the door opened. An elderly male boarder stood in his nightgown and cap, holding a candle, asking if she were all right.

"Yes, I got locked in by mistake." She took the key from the lock. Thank goodness whoever had locked her in had left it there, and shut the door again, apologizing for disturbing everybody, for a few people had appeared like pale ghosts upon the staircase and landing.

The house settled down again, and a few minutes later, Emma emerged from her room, tightly wrapped in her cloak, and made her way to the front door. She opened it and went out, looking about her as she did. When outside, she could see another light bobbing nearby and heard low voices. She had to get away. She began to run as quietly as she could but inevitably made a noise. Footsteps hurried after her, men's footsteps, and her heart lurched as a light fell upon her. She ran down the back path in the direction of the river. The moon came out from behind the clouds, and she saw the grassy bank. She climbed over it and desperately wondered where she could hide.

There was the half-stripped skeleton of an old barge on a green verge adjacent to the mud, and Emma hid behind it. She could see the light bobbing, but then a curse and darkness. She heard grunts of frustration. What was he doing? Was he injured? Then she heard the squelch of footsteps in the mud. This time they became fainter until all was quiet. Wrapped in her cloak, she must have fallen asleep sitting up against the rotting hull.

The mud lark's voices told her that they were up and about with the dawn breaking. They were delighted about something. When she raised her head, she saw that they had found some items on the beach, presumably where her pursuer had fallen and lost the change in his pockets.

They were examining something.

"Oooh, miss!" They made as if to run from her, but she called out to them. "Stop a minute! I want to give you money for your dinner." She took out her reticule and they neared her, looking at one another.

"What have you got in your 'and?" she asked pleasantly to the boy who had something hidden behind his back. "Please can I 'ave a look?" she asked.

He drew his hand out, producing a curved dagger with a fancy, old-fashioned handle.

"I said I'd give you money for your dinner, so 'ere," she said. "This'll buy you lots of dinners! But give me that."

She dispensed several silver coins and hid the knife under her cloak as she left.

THE DAGGER

"Emma, I want to know what happened last night and why you ran away!"

Mrs. Howard stood before her on the rough path leading from the inlet, blocking her way, indignant. Was this an act, or was she innocent?

"You locked me in my room!" she said angrily.

"It wasn't me! Another thing. Have you seen Tilly? The boarders had to go out without breakfast this morning!"

"No, I 'aven't seen Tilly."

"Why are you so muddy? What 'appened, Emma?"

"I got free from the room, and I ran off, down 'ere, and some blighter followed me and I 'ad to hide! Please tell me everyfink you know about the smugglers, Mrs. Howard. You told me once that you get tea cheap, and I understood it was contraband. I 'ave to save Pat. You must know somefink! Please!"

"Come back to the house, Emma, and I will tell you all I know."

"No, I'm not going back up there, sorry."

"Very well then!" Mrs. Howard sounded angry as she turned on her heel.

Emma pulled her hood up to conceal her face and leaned against a tree trunk at the edge of the bank. From there she could see anybody who was about to walk the muddy, marshy flats.

Mrs. Howard hurried back to the house, while Emma kept watch for the man who lost the dagger to return for it. She did not have to wait very long. She spied a short, thin man walking up to the place where the knife had been found, his eyes upon the mud, his cloak flapping behind him in his rush to cover the ground.

She gasped suddenly, for the figure was familiar. Who was it who had the odd flat cap with the green plume?

Mr. Mortimer!

She had not seen his face, but she was sure. The man who had acted as her cousin, who had been a part of her downfall into ruin and ill-health. He could see her at any moment.

She saw him speak with the mud larks. It was time for her to go. For a few extra pennies, the poor little ones would tell him all. She would have to try to slip away, and the only route was toward the Howard house again.

One of the urchins pointed her out, and she was now being pursued. He could run faster than she, who was impeded by her long mud-soaked skirts, and he caught her and reaching under her cloak, retrieved his dagger and raised it above his head as if to strike. Emma screamed. She was sure she would be killed there and then, but a woman's voice called "Stop!" and he lowered it.

"Bring her up here!" she heard Mrs. Howard say.

He dragged her in the direction of the house. She was pushed in the back door, and Mrs. Howard was in the kitchen, her face flushed and anxious.

"You're a fool, Mortimer," she said, "Not that way, with *claret* spilled everywhere. Perhaps you would drop another handkerchief, too. Now put her in your own apartment."

"Mrs. Howard, why?" Emma gasped out.

"It's your own fault!" was the tight-lipped answer. Emma was very grieved. Mrs. Howard had been good to her at one time. She had taken her in, sheltered her, and given her an occupation. What had happened to her?

"Everybody has gone out to work. Secure her, but there is no need to gag her," Mrs. Howard said as she took the poker and began to stoke the fire as if it were an ordinary day.

Mortimer dragged her away. He was surprisingly strong for his neat frame, and he dragged her up the stairs and into his own rooms, the place of her undoing and of all of her trouble.

"You played a cruel trick upon me!" Emma shot out to him as he shoved her onto a hard chair. "I suppose you know that Dudley is dead?"

His expression told her that he had not known, so she went on, "He repented before he died. I hope you do too because Hell is real. Let me go, Mortimer."

"You fell for it all so easily." He smiled a cruel smile. "Take me to me grandmovver!" he mimicked her, in a falsetto.

"You won't laugh someday, no you won't. I 'ope it won't be too late for you."

He ignored her and bound her hands and feet.

"What's going on?" A female voice was heard from the bedchamber. Mortimer went in, shut the door, and spoke to somebody at length. Then he came back and left the apartment.

Emma was struggling to get out of her bonds. Once again, she had not heeded Patrick's advice and had relied upon her own will. Was there any hope now of freeing him?

TILLY

Tilly emerged from the bedchamber wearing a man's dressing gown. "Oh, Emma. You know too much," she said with sorrow.

"Tilly! Was it you locked me into my room?"

"Yes, that was me." Tilly threw herself onto the sofa and threw her feet on the back of it, one foot resting on the other. "I'm not really a maid."

"So I see." Emma could not help the sarcastic tone.

"I'm Mrs. Mortimer."

"So you don't live in that 'orrible attic room then?"

"Oh no. Not at all." She giggled and sat up straight again. "Mrs. Howard doesn't know! She's looking for me at this moment, I bet she is. Oh, look, she's going out!" Tilly raised her head to peer out the window. "She's going to the village to look for me!"

"Tilly, why don't you tell me what's going on?" Emma said desperately. "Mrs. Howard is up to her eyes in something, isn't she?"

"I suppose it's no 'arm to tell you, because Morty won't let you live beyond today," Tilly said sadly. "You shouldn't have come back, Emma." She picked up a mirror that was lying on the table and began to gaze at herself. Emma noticed that her hands were rough and her nails short and cracked. She was close enough to see that there was no wedding ring, nor was there a ring mark on her finger.

"So it's all my fault?" she asked her, for the moment keeping her observations to herself.

"Yes, because last night, Mrs. Howard told me that a long time ago you saw Mr. Hodges at the tobacconist. She's a friend of the tobacconist and went to tell him to be more careful, but she smoothed things over with him as far as you were concerned, said you were no danger to their operation, and so on. So they left you alone. But Mrs. Howard was drawn back into the smuggling then, she wanted nice things, cheap or for nothing, and Bertie said if he could use this house as a safe house for merchandise, that she could 'ave her cut."

"Where does Mr. Mortimer come into all this? When did he come to live here again?"

"After the last tenants left, he come back. Everybody leaves except 'im cos of the spooks. So when he come back, she took 'im in, for she couldn't let to nobody else. Then he found out about the smugglin'. He's going to be a famous actor, but until then, he needs money to live, cos a horrid uncle cut 'im off. So he got involved. His job is to find good-paying customers for the stuff, for those that were paying, weren't paying enough. His theatre friends like nice old-fashioned things, paintings and suchlike."

"I thought smuggling was about tobacco and spirits."

"Not with Mortimer! Now they deal in very expensive *objay darr*."

"What's *objay darr*?"

"What is it? Objects of Art! It's French! I could show you candlesticks from Venice. That's in Italy," she added helpfully.

"And you, Tilly? Why do you have to act as maid when you're his wife?"

She laughed suddenly. "Cos Morty says these wealthy ladies he does business with are in love wi' 'im!"

"So who really does the housework?"

"A village girl, she comes and goes," Tilly said vaguely, waving one coarse hand in the air. "I do the breakfasts, but I got tired of it, very tired of it, and this morning I said to myself that I've 'ad enough so I went back to sleep!"

"And you sleep here when Mrs. Howard thinks you sleep in the attic room?"

"Yes, of course! I goes up there to make it look like I live there but I don't."

"Who went out last night after my door was locked?"

"Morty. He went to tell the Growler, Bertie's friend. He was bringin' him back here cos Morty didn't know what to do with you."

"Why was Mr. Hodges murdered?"

"He objected to the *objay darr* and wanted 'em to stay in spirits and tobacco. He thought the police turn a blind eye to cheap items but if you steal from rich people, they come lookin' and the police look 'arder cos of the rewards they get. Hodges began to threaten Mortimer."

"Did Mortimer kill him?" Emma was sure from what Mrs. Howard had said, but if she escaped from here, she would need Tilly's cooperation to clear Patrick's name.

Tilly made no reply.

"You can tell me," she said encouragingly, "since you said I'll be dead by sunset."

"All right then, he did."

"All by himself? Hodges was a big man."

"The Growler, and Bertie."

"An innocent man 'as been arrested for that murder."

Tilly put down the mirror, got up, and paced about the room.

"I'm sorry about that."

"But he will be freed soon, and you should be sorry for yourself, for after all this is over, the police will catch up with you. Are you really Mrs. Mortimer?"

Tilly looked at her sharply. "Of course I am, or will be soon." She held up her left hand and inspected it as if a sparkling ring were on the finger already.

"These rooms have an evil, deceitful spirit," Emma said. "Have you felt it?"

Tilly looked about her and shivered a little. Emma chose her next words carefully.

"I was an innocent girl when I stepped into these rooms many years ago. Your lover deceived me."

"Mortimer and you!"

Emma allowed her to think the worst for the moment. "I got a horrid disease from my encounter, and I almost died. The foul ward, in the workhouse, was where I ended up. Two long years of brutal treatment with mercury. It's where servants go when they get a secret disease that they can't tell anybody about. Oh, Tilly, I see so much of myself in you! What age are you, Tilly?"

Tilly looked frightened now.

"I'm sixteen."

"He'll never marry you, Tilly. You're the maid. I see your 'ands, rough and cracked like mine from scrubbing those back steps. Gentlemen don't marry maids. I don't want you to end up like me! If you only knew my suffering!"

Tilly took a step backwards. Her face was unhappy.

"If you turn Queen's evidence, you won't be prosecuted; otherwise if they think you 'ad something to do with the murder, you could be hanged too! Mr. Moore has engaged a powerful barrister to defend 'im and he knows that I was coming 'ere. If I don't report back to 'im today, he's going to look for me 'ere. He'll send the police, and you'll all be arrested."

Matilda was shaking now.

"I was good to you, Tilly. Remember? Please untie me and let me out. I swear I will attest to the fact that you helped me, and I will plead for you. Where's Morty now?"

"He's gone to audition. 'e wants to play a murderer, some geezer called Ofello."

"He was practisin' on me earlier, maybe. Come on, Tilly, untie me. We'll go from 'ere. This is a bad place."

The girl came forward and loosened her bonds. She was trembling and weeping.

Emma rubbed her sore wrists and ankles. "Now I'm going, and you can come with me. You see, I mean what I said. Get some clothes on you quick, and we'll go."

She could hardly wait for the girl to dress herself, so impatient was she, but she did so in record time, and they ran downstairs and out the front door, up the laneway and through the back streets towards the tube station. She and Emma boarded a train to take them to Chancery Lane where Mr. Weekes' office was.

On the tube, Tilly began to talk.

"So Morty doesn't love me. I wondered why he wouldn't introduce me to his mother and sister when they visited him last week. I brought them up tea and scones and do you know 'e never said a word. Not a word. He said to me after that it was because the time wasn't right yet. But I think 'e might have said *somefink*. I stood around after setting the tray down and smiled a bit and he said, *'that's all right, Tilly. I'll pull the bell if I need you.'* So I felt dismissed. That did make me think."

"He's also a murderer, Tilly," Emma reminded her.

"Ooh, yes, that should've been enough to put me off him. But he made me promises. Will I ever meet a nice bloke, Emma?"

"Tilly, you're sixteen years old. You haven't even reached your peak in beauty yet."

"Will you continue to be my friend, Emma?"

"Course I will. I'll go back to sellin' fish an' you can 'elp me."

Emma told her more of her own story, including the information that it had not been Mortimer that had seduced her, but he had tricked her most cruelly into going to a place where her ruin had been planned.

"He as good as did it," was Tilly's reply. "He's a bad man."

They were nearing Chancery Lane.

"Now it's fancy in 'ere. Don't get cold feet; stick to your story," Emma lectured her.

She did as asked, and Mr. Weekes promised to do all he could to drop any charges against her if she testified against the Hammersmith gang. He was amused to see the ring. He'd pressed it on his cousin, but he had secretly wished it for his daughter. Yes, it would cover all expenses of setting Mr. Moore free. They were to return in two days.

Emma left, and spending almost all of the money she had, she booked a room for both of them in a cheap lodging house in Spitalfields. She would go and buy fish in the morning and sell it as she used to.

FREEDOM

"**M**r. Moore is to be freed." The note from Mr. Weekes was the sweetest gift to Emma. She hurried to Newgate prison and there awaited him outside the gate.

Oh, so many came out, and none of them was the face and figure she so wished to see! But after waiting about two hours, at last the beloved familiar face appeared, and Patrick Moore stepped into freedom.

He looked about and saw her, smiling, beaming.

"Emma!" He rushed to her side. "Oh, those dimples, how I love 'em."

"I have you to thank, I believe," he went on with relief. "And the miss who's willing to testify against the gang. They're in custody, most of 'em. Where is she?"

"She's at my fish stall. She doesn't know one fish from another so I will 'ave to go back there soon. Was it very 'orrid in there?"

"Oh, beyond anything. I was in a cell with thirty other men. Filthy. Smelly. Dangerous too. Food was inedible. Ah, fresh air!" He looked about him, not minding the infernal, constant fog from the river.

"Were you manacled all the time?"

"No, not when the cell door was locked. A few of the violent prisoners were chained though. By the way, you promised you would tell me something, and I've been in suspense since you mentioned it."

"Yes, I did. And I will keep my promise."

As they walked along, she told him all. The opium, the foul ward, the mercury. And how she may always be having the after-effects of the treatment: aches, pains, sick stomach.

"I knew you'd been mishandled by that scoundrel. But you're cured of the disease, Emma, aren't you? You can't pass it on if you're cured. Is that what you're afraid of?"

"No," said Emma quietly. "Pat, I can't have children. Mercury makes a person sterile. And I may be ill sometimes, and I may not live to old age. All this was told to me."

There was a few moments silence.

"Is that the reason you don't want to marry? The children part?"

"Yes. I know you want children."

There was another pause. Emma's heart began to drop. She had been beginning to hope that it would not matter.

"We'll have nieces and nephews, Emma. All livin' around us, and in and out of our

'ouse! I have twelve already, and in ten years, I expect we'll have twenty-four! It's not that bad. And only God knows how long your or my life will be. We'll take the bad with the good and 'ope for the best."

"Please think about the children for a while, Patrick. It's that important, it is. I can endure it if you'd rather marry somebody else. Don't say anyfink now. Wait as long as you like. You can find me at the fish market at Spitalfields."

"But I know already, Emma."

"No, Patrick. I want you to fink about it. Then I'll be easy."

They parted, but not before a very warm embrace was shared in the middle of the street, to the amusement of some onlookers and the disgust of others who felt that public displays of affection were vulgar.

It was only three days later that Patrick appeared at the stall, smiling.

"Seven 'addock, ten pounds of skate, and a ton of eels, and Emma could you please name the day? I only delayed these three days to please you."

"Oh, Pat!" Her hands were all fishy, so she could not reach out to touch him. "Just wait a moment -" She dealt with the customers as fast as she could, and Tilly told her she could manage if she wanted to go for a while.

Emma washed her hands under the standpipe and borrowed a bottle of vanilla essence from another costermonger and sprinkled it on her hands.

"There, now I don't stink anymore. Will we walk?"

"Is there a nice place to walk to?"

"No, not 'ere. We're not Belgravia!"

"Just up there then, where there's a waste patch. Oh, it's a dump, but never mind, it's quiet here. Look, poppies!"

The ugly pile of earth had brought forth bright orange poppies, and they were in bloom. They rippled and swayed all together in the breeze.

"See how 'appy they are, Emma! They're as 'appy as if they'd been grown in Kew Gardens and not this place."

"I no longer 'anker after things beyond me, Pat. It's a gift to be content."

"I'm glad to 'ear that, love. I'll have to get another job though."

"And I'll work, Pat. But it has to be somefink I find some satisfaction in."

"You don't have to work, love. My wife won't have to work."

"Patrick, one fink worries me. Your family. They can't approve of me now."

"Emma, I 'aven't said one word to them."

"About my disease?"

"They don't even know about 'ow you was tricked and drugged. I never told 'em. I knew it couldn't be your fault. They think you went away sudden to find your relations. That's all."

"Thank you, Pat. I didn't deserve you being so mindful of me. I thought after the time you met me in the hotel, that time, that you had lost all respect for me and thrown my reputation to the winds. I deserved it, for I stayed willin'ly with him."

"Let's not go back to that evenin', love."

"I had to learn my lesson and learn what is important. Jesus is first in my life now. I was broken; He rescued me. First through His words, that Christmas day in the foul ward, I was sure I was dying. He came! He came to us in the foul ward! Next, through the people who looked after me there, because without the parish, I would've died on the streets. And much more. I 'ad no time for Him, He left me to myself and my own stubborn way, and I fell very far indeed. I bitterly regretted what I did."

"Stop berating yourself; you were drugged. What did 'appen that letter I sent to Norland Square warning you? It should 'ave arrived on the Saturday."

"Per'aps Hensley set it aside. He was gettin' annoyed delivering letters to me."

He pressed her hand. "Let's marry soon. Mrs. Hodges has agreed to give me my designs back." He told her the story of the fount he had designed and lost to Hodges.

"If only you could make an' sell it, Pat! It would be a good start."

"That needs capital. Emma, leave your lodgings and move in with us until the wedding."

"What about Tilly? I can't leave 'er."

Mrs. Moore welcomed her back, and so grateful was she to Emma that she welcomed her little friend too.

RIVERSEDGE IN RUINS

Mrs. Howard had evaded arrest, and her house, *Riversedge*, burned down before the police had searched it. She was nowhere to be found, nor were any remains discovered in the ashes. It was rumoured that she left by boat that moonlit night, that the rich people whose names were associated with the smuggling compensated her greatly, and she began a new life as someone else in another part of the country. The local people claimed that an evil spirit had set the house afire.

The mud larks were out of work, for the barges stopped there no more, and there was little to be found. Some were taken in by the parish or sent to orphanages. In time, the birds were the only sign of life around the charred remains of Riversedge House and the lonely laneway that led to it.

Patrick's arrest reported in the London dailies was seen by many people, and two men who lived at Norland Square were very much affected. Rupert Carmichael was one. It brought the events of that winter back to him. He could bear the secret no longer, and so he confided in a person he considered to be a friend from his childhood, an upper servant at his home, the butler Mr. Hensley. He descended to the pantry one evening to pour out his heart.

"I saw the arrest also," Hensley said. How he too regretted not passing on the letter and felt wretched. He had not known the whole of it though, only that Mrs. Bowles was supposed to accompany Emma somewhere, and that meant she had not run off with Mr. Pond, as was commonly thought. Now he learned from the young master that a nefarious trick had been played on the girl for a wager. Where was she now? Had she sunk into the filthy streets and lived now by prostitution? His remorse became acute. That night, sleep eluded him, and the matter preyed upon his mind for days, pushing the other, his recent diagnosis, to the back of his mind.

Then he read that Patrick had been released and that a gang working out of Hammersmith had been rounded up. Patrick Moore was innocent.

I can't do anything for Emma, he thought. *But I can do something for the lad. I can't get his sweetheart back for him, but I can give him another start.*

He had considerable savings from a lifetime of service and frugality which were intended for his retirement, but having been recently diagnosed with cancer, he knew he would not live to enjoy his money. He had never taken even five pounds from the fund, but now he withdrew five hundred. It was not difficult to find Patrick's address; a half-crown to a reporter at the London Times produced it the following day.

WINDFALL

"Patrick, this is for you, just delivered by a cabman. He came to the door with it, but I'm sure there's someone inside the cab." A wondering Mrs. Moore gave him a small packet. There was a thick envelope stuffed with money inside, and a note.

Mr. Moore. This is conscience money. Please make no enquiry where it came from. I wish you every success.

Patrick dashed out, but the cab had already clattered off.

He could not wait to show it to Emma that evening when she returned from her fish stall so he went immediately to tell her. Together they speculated who it could be, but though they discussed it on and off for months, even years, they never found out.

Mrs. Hodges wished to sell the foundry. She had no idea about her husband's other life, but she was deeply in debt and very fearful of her future. Patrick offered to buy it, and they came to an acceptable arrangement, whereby she would get an annuity. Patrick began to manufacture his own metal font, now named *'Emma Ornamental,'* and it took off, so he soon was able to buy a house with three rooms upstairs and three downstairs.

Emma became Mrs. Moore soon after that, and the couple were so happy that even the court case at the Old Bailey hardly disturbed them. Mr. Philip Mortimer had a successful audition that day for the part of the villain Othello but had returned to Riversedge only to be arrested there for a real murder. In his conceited state, he had regaled the police as to how he did it. He was sentenced to hang, but his wealthy friends intervened, and he spent the rest of his life in prison. Whether he repented of his actions on the long hours picking oakum or on the treadmill, nobody knows, but it is hoped that in the dark prison he cried out for salvation and ended his days peacefully.

The other culprits denied any involvement in the murder of Mr. Hodges, and there was not enough evidence to convict them of it, but they got 10 years each for smuggling.

CHRISTMAS CHILD

Seven Years Later

It was Christmas. All was jollity in the Moore extended household, for there were enough grandchildren tumbling over each other to produce all kinds of joy and expectation, baking and preparation. The cribs were taken out and put up to show the children that this season was about the coming of Jesus, and it was His birthday, and the children sang carols in front of the little figures of Jesus, Mary, Joseph, the shepherds, and the lambs. Then they sat in front of the Christmas tree and watched the decorations twinkle, and anticipated when the bonbons hanging from it would be taken down and be placed into their little hands.

Some of the Moore's adult children and their children would come together on Christmas Day. Those who were absent were with their in-laws.

"Thank God nobody emigrated, or even went to live in the north! How I'd miss them, Jimmy!"

"I love to see 'em coming in, and I love to see 'em going home," Mr. Moore said, smiling as he lit his pipe.

"Yes, indeed, for we need a bit of peace and quiet! Hasn't God blessed us all, except for poor Pat and Emma? Seven years, and no children. I keep askin' myself what could be wrong?"

"Not every couple 'as a flock of dustbin lids, Mary."

"Yes, but I know Pat would love them, but Emma is sickly, poor thing. Maybe that has something to do with it. My poor son would love to be a Papa."

"He doesn't seem to mind at all."

"How do you know?"

"I asked him one time. He said he didn't mind, that he 'ad nieces and nephews enough to satisfy 'em both, and hardly a week passes but they 'aven't one or two to stay over with them."

"That's true, luv. They are very popular with 'em too. And I think he's helped out poor John and Lucy once or twice."

Lucy's husband had been injured in an accident and could not work much.

"More than that, he wants to keep their young Paddy in school and send him to university, for he's very bright. He wants 'im to do law."

"How do you know all this, Jimmy Moore?" His wife sounded annoyed. "Your long walks with him, I suppose!" She drew back the lace curtain and peered out the window. "Oh, look at that white sky. There's snow in it! And here's Ollie and Tilly and the baby! And just behind 'em, John with his brood!"

Soon their quiet kitchen was filled with merriment and children rushing to their grandparents to show them what presents they had found in their stockings. Oranges, raisins, little toy donkeys and horses and dolls were all presented for admiration. Other families arrived, and soon the house was swarming.

"Where's Patrick?" Mrs. Moore wanted to know when Mary and her family arrived, for they lived in the same street as Pat and Emma.

"Emma's unwell today. In fact, Pat is getting the doctor, he's so worried about her. She's abed, with no energy to get up. And her father is coming to stay tomorrow."

Dick Brown had spent only a month in America. He missed his daughter. But it had not been a wasted trip; he'd arranged a match between his cabin mate Mr. Prout and Miss Weekes after he found out that he, too, was a teacher and wished to start a school in Oregon. He told his daughter that as a mark of gratitude, Mr. Prout had bestowed his silver fob watch upon him. Emma chose to believe him. Dick had returned and charmed and married a widow who was comfortably off.

"Oh, poor Emma, and at Christmas too! Tilly, if you want to feed the baby, take her into the sitting room. There's a nice fire there and a bit of peace."

"Oh, thanks, Mum." Tilly beamed. She had been absorbed into the Moore family as soon as Ollie had laid eyes upon her. Tilly had taken her time about saying 'yes,' and Ollie had waited. Baby Emma followed a year later.

A few streets away, Patrick watched out for the doctor with a sick heart and opened the door to him before he had knocked. He waited anxiously downstairs, pacing. Emma had been very sick of late. She said she felt different; something had changed, she said, and she feared the worst, for mercury could cause an early death. Her stomach had swollen. "If it's my liver, like poor Ruth I looked after in the foul ward, I haven't got long, Pat. Her stomach was like this, only worse. You may well have to learn to live without me. I don't want to talk like this, but I told you this could happen. I'm trying to prepare you for the worst."

The doctor seemed to take a long time upstairs. What was going on? Was it serious? He rested his head on the banister with growing agitation. Finally, the door opened and shut, and Dr. Piggott descended the stair.

"What is it? Tell me. She was very ill some years ago. I thought it might have flared up again."

"Oh, yes, she told me her history, because we had quite an argument up there in the room, but I'm positive I'm correct. I even heard it with my little trumpet!" He held up a little instrument, wagging it in the air.

"What, Doctor? What did you hear?"

"A heartbeat not her own, Pat. That's why she's been sick. Her womb is enlarged to about four months now. In five months, which I calculate to be around the end of May, you'll be the father of a bouncing baby. Incredible, yes. We doctors are scientists, but we are fools if we don't believe in the odd miracle now and then. They keep us humble, you know. You and Mrs. Moore have one."

"A - a child!" Patrick gasped.

"You had better go up and congratulate her, Pat." The doctor was smiling. "This makes my Christmas," he said as he left. "Ah, look at the snow falling! Life is good!"

Pat needed no second urging. He took the twelve steps in three bounds. Upstairs, Emma had a serene smile. Her eyes were looking up to Heaven.

"Our Christmas miracle, Pat. Our Christmas miracle."

Soon a visitor appeared from his mother's house to enquire about Emma, and there was no need to conceal the news. There was great rejoicing that night, and carols and songs were sung with extra love and gratitude, for on this snowy Christmas Day God had sent to the Moore family 'Tidings of Great Joy'.

THANK YOU FOR CHOOSING A PUREREAD BOOK!

We hope you enjoyed the story, and as a way to thank you for choosing PureRead we'd like to send you this free book, and other fun reader rewards…

Click here for your free copy of Whitechapel Waif
PureRead.com/victorian

Thanks again for reading.
See you soon!

LOVE VICTORIAN CHRISTMAS SAGA ROMANCE?

If you enjoyed this story why not continue straight away with other books in our PureRead Victorian Christmas Romance library?

Read them all...

Churchyard Orphan

Orphan Christmas Miracle

Workhouse Girl's Christmas Dream

The Winter Widow's Daughter

The Match Girl & The Lost Boy's Christmas Hope

The Christmas Convent Child

The Orphan Girl's Winter Secret

Rag And Bone Winter Hope

Isadora's Christmas Plight

HAVE YOU READ

ORPHAN CHRISTMAS MIRACLE

I'm certain that Emma and Patrick's story has warmed your heart today? What an emotional ride to their happy every after!

I would also love to introduce you to another thrilling Christmas story, this time telling the tale of little Mae Chester.

Mae Chester, the Christmas miracle girl, loses her parents at a very tender age and is reluctantly received by her loveless uncle. Cold and unforgiving, he makes no secret of his disdain for the waiflike child. It is only Mae's friendship with the boy next door that keeps hope alive in her heart.

As Mae and Hubert, her neighbour and faithful friend, grow, so does their love and affection for one another, until forces beyond their control separate them in the cruellest way possible.

It will take a miracle and many long years for the two lovers to find each other again.

For your enjoyment here are the first chapters of Mae's story…

It begins on a bright day in Spring on the Patterson Estate, Sheffield County, England

The church bells tolled continuously on that warm Saturday at the beginning of spring. The flowers were in full bloom around the estate and the small village chapel was filled with the scent of roses. Servants had filled every free space with vases of blooming white and red roses, hence the sweet scent. Villagers came out in droves and lined the road from the estate gate right to the small chapel in the middle of the square. Everyone was very eager to catch a glimpse of the procession that was slowly making its way from the large manor, down the road and to the chapel, for it was a very fancy sight indeed.

As patrons of the village, one of the gifts that the Patterson family had given to the small church was a medium sized second-hand organ, and melodious sounds were heard by those standing close to the chapel. It was clear that a skilled organist had been brought in, no doubt to make this day very special indeed, for none of the inhabitants of Patterson Village had ever heard such magnificent playing before. Clearly, Mr. Patterson had gone all out to make sure that this day would go down in the annals of Patterson Village history as the wedding of the century.

For on this bright Saturday morning, the spinster daughter of the lord of the manor was preparing to tie the knot. It wasn't that Patterson Village, named after the family that owned the estate, hadn't seen weddings before. If ever there was a village in Sheffield that boasted of its many nuptials in spring and summer, indeed Patterson was it.

This was a different kind of wedding, for the thirty-year-old spinster, never before known to be interested in matrimony, was wedding a much unexpected groom. This man was the estate's twenty-four-year-old gardener. Tongues wagged, and speculation was rife as to why the simple Edwin Cameron, son of the poor widow, Mrs. Grace Cameron, could have reached above his estate to consent to a wedding with a woman who was clearly his superior in every way. The rumour was that the young man would be dropping his own simple surname to take up the more prestigious one of his bride.

In the leading carriage of the procession, a middle-aged woman sat sobbing quietly in one corner, using the corner of her frayed shawl to wipe her face from time to time. The intended groom was the only other occupant of the carriage. Though his face was devoid of any expression, his gentle soul was bleeding because of his Mama's heart wrenching sobs.

"Ma, you've got to stop crying, for you'll make yourself ill," Edwin Cameron pleaded with his mother in a gentle voice. "You know that if there was any other way, I wouldn't be doing this."

"If only your father hadn't died and left us destitute and heavily in debt," Mrs. Cameron sniffed. "It breaks my heart to see my only son sacrificing his happiness just because his father was a heavy gambler."

"Mama, please don't distress yourself. Mr. Patterson said it's going to be a marriage in name only, and after two years have passed, Miss Elaine Patterson and I will go our separate ways. Then I can go and marry for love, after saving our home and name from ruin." He didn't tell his mother about the conversation he'd overheard between Mr. Patterson and his daughter, one in which an heir had been mentioned. Miss Elaine had brushed her father aside and told him that she had no desire to bear any child and was only getting married to fulfil the terms of her grandfather's will. The thought had troubled him for days because he couldn't imagine siring a child with the cold and hard Miss Elaine Patterson.

That she'd chosen him to be her husband had surprised even him, but then he'd decided to use the strange union to his advantage also. All his father's debts would be settled, and his mother would live as a free woman for the rest of her life. No price was too high to pay to ensure that his beloved mother never spent another sleepless night. Yet he made no mention of this to his distraught mother, instead seeking to reassure her. "Ma, all will be will, you'll see. Mr. Patterson is a man of his word."

But Mrs. Cameron was shaking her head. "Don't believe everything that those people tell you," she whispered urgently. "Right now, they hold our lives in their hands, and they can so easily change the terms of the agreement. I fear that you, my son, may be walking into a trap that you won't be able to extricate yourself from. There's more to all this than meets the eye, and my heart is full of fear, Son." She fell on her knees before him, and he quickly raised her back to the seat. "It's not too late to change your mind."

"Ma, I can't let you go to the debtors' prison or even the poor workhouse. This is the only way that I'll be able to keep you safe. It's a marriage of convenience, and besides, Miss Elaine doesn't even look at me. I'm merely a means to an end for her. Please," he wiped her tears, "Don't cry,

Ma, you're breaking my heart." His voice cracked with emotion, and his face was quite pale.

Mrs. Cameron saw the distress on her son's face and quickly wiped her face. Her love for her son overshadowed the distress she was feeling. From the moment he was born, Edwin had been the light of her life, and seeing him this distraught nearly broke her heart. He'd always been a good and obedient son, and he shouldn't have to pay for the sins of his father. He always took too much upon his own shoulders. Whenever she had tried to stop him from overdoing things, he would tell her that as the man of the home, it was expected of him. Now he was shouldering yet another burden that wasn't of his making, that of ensuring that she didn't end up homeless or in a poor workhouse.

"See, I'm not crying anymore," she gave him a shaky smile. "I pray that all will be well with you in your new marriage, my son. But never let your guard down, not even for one moment. Always watch yourself around these people. Don't acquire a taste for their delicacies and never forget where you came from. You, my son, are a worthy man. Please don't trust these people too much. We come from different stations in life, and I want you to always know your place."

Though the young man knew that his mother spoke the truth, he was determined to go through with this wedding. He had no love for Miss Elaine Patterson, for she was an arrogant woman who had shunned many a suitor. Everyone said that her only true love was the estate that her ancestors had built up decades ago. The Pattersons' unquestionable and firm loyalty to the House of Hanover had seen them reaping vast benefits over many decades, and it was still as strong as ever. The only regret, the current Lord of the Manor was often heard to say, was that he had no male children to carry on his name.

Many felt that perhaps that was the reason that Miss Elaine Patterson strove to prove to her father that she was better than seven sons. The estate was the love of her life. She gave her all to it, and it prospered in her hands. It was therefore surprising that she had actually agreed to get married, and to a man who was considered to be a nobody, at that. But given that the man was going to change his name for her, it stood to reason that an heir was desired, a male one, who would continue carrying the Patterson name.

All these thoughts were in the minds of the villagers as they watched the wedding ceremony from afar. None of the villagers were invited to the fancy feast held at the manor afterwards, but it was piped abroad that the fare that was spread for the dozens of nobles and gentry who were invited, was enough to feed half of England for a full year. The festivities would go on for a full week!

Edwin watched as his bride walked down the aisle on her father's arm, and he felt nothing but deadness inside. This was the price he was willing to pay to keep his mother safe. There was nothing he wouldn't do for his mother. Miss Elaine Patterson looked radiant in her beautiful haute couture wedding gown, made especially for her by a Parisian designer. She carried a large bouquet of bright red roses from the garden that Edwin so carefully tended to, and this was the only gift he'd given her. He just wanted the day to be over so he could go back to his lovely roses that never judged or criticized him as his soon to be wife was doing even now with her cold grey eyes through the light veil that covered her face.

Same Day in Spring, Hundreds of Miles Away

Ravenscroft Village, Pembroke, Wales

The small village chapel was nearly empty, and only a handful of people sat in the old wooden pews. Some of the pews were even broken down, but it didn't matter, since there weren't enough souls in the chapel that day to fill them. There were no flowers and no choir lined up close to the ancient piano ready to sing the wedding march. There was not a carriage in sight, nor did the church bells toll on that warm Saturday morning in spring. To everyone around, it was just an ordinary Saturday morning, just like any other, but to two people, it was a very special day indeed.

Clive Chester slipped into the chapel through the side door and made his way to the altar where the cloaked vicar was waiting. The bridegroom smiled at his widowed father and waved to Mrs. Burns, who was his employer. Mrs. Burns was the village fishmonger's wife, and she'd taken over the fledgling business when her drunken husband broke his neck one evening after drinking heavily and climbing onto a scaffold to prove his prowess as a flying human being. The ground on which he'd landed proved victorious, and thus Mrs. Ethel Burns became a widow and the proprietor of Burns Fishmongers.

Clive's heart was beating very fast, and his eyes were glued to the main chapel door. His clothes were a size too large for him, but he wore the hand-me-down suit, a rare loan from his employer, with much pride, and he'd decked himself out best as he could. He still couldn't believe that Mrs. Burns, in a rare show of generosity, had decided to loan him one of her dead husband's Sunday suits, and even a pair of shoes, as well as the starched shirt and cravat. Everything Clive wore on his wedding day had once belonged to the late Mr. Burns.

A shadow fell over the door he was gazing at, and Clive's breath caught in his throat. For there at the doorway stood the most beautiful woman in the world to him.

"Ashley," he whispered, love shining on his face and making his eyes glow.

Ashley Reid raised her head and smiled, even though she couldn't see the face of her beloved through the thick veil that covered hers. It was discoloured with age, but she wore it with pride, as she did the unsightly gown that had been taken in too many times over the years, so much that it had lost its original shape. Many brides of her family had worn the dress that Cousin Morgan insisted had been given to its first wearer by Queen Victoria's grandmother herself. How true that legend was, no one could tell, but every bride that had come before Ashley had the dress altered to suit her as needed, and it was worn with pride.

Like the thick veil, also a gift from the Queen's grandmother, the gown was discoloured because of being washed too many times and from poor storage. The collar and edges of the sleeves were frayed, but Ashley, a good seamstress, had done her best to make it presentable. Perhaps its best features were the sparkling white flat pearl buttons that ran from the neck right down to the floor, and it had surprised Ashley that all the dress's original buttons were still intact.

As Ashley glided down the aisle to the man she had loved for so long, she purposed in her heart that all her daughters would wear the gown and the veil. For legend had it that every woman who wore it had a happy marriage, so she was very careful because the fabric was delicate. Yes, she would keep it safely until her own daughters wore it one day.

The moment she arrived at the altar, she heard Clive breathe in relief, and she knew that he'd been under a lot of tension leading to this day. It wasn't easy being the only son of a man who expected him to marry well, but Clive had chosen her and forsaken many others worthier than she was. This was special grace, and in that moment, as he held out his hand and she placed hers in it, she prayed that she would be a good wife to him.

Clive felt Ashley's hand trembling in his and he squeezed it gently, reminding her that he was by her side. He loved this woman with his whole heart, and even facing much opposition from his family hadn't moved him to change his mind about marrying her. Theirs was a large family and to all intents, the church should have been filled with his relatives, but because he'd refused to marry the daughter of the wealthiest man in their village, most of them had stayed away. They thought he was throwing his life away by marrying a woman who had no prospects in life and came from a very poor family. But she was the love of his life and nothing else mattered. After giving her hand another squeeze, he turned and faced the vicar, ready to say the vows that would bind him to Ashley Reid for the rest of his life.

"Dearly beloved...," the vicar's voice boomed in the near-empty chapel. The sermon was long and boring, and Clive was thankful that they had to stand through it because he was afraid that he might have fallen asleep had he been seated.

"And now you may face your bride," Clive felt Ashley nudging him and he blinked.

"What is it?" He whispered.

"My veil, remove it," she instructed from the side of her lips. Clive did as bidden, and when he looked into the eyes of the woman he loved above all else, it was as if time stood still. Ashley felt very shy at the intensity in Clive's eyes, but she couldn't look away from him either. Everything else faded away, and in that moment all that was left was just the two of them.

Whatever else the vicar said passed above the heads of the two lovers who were completely lost in their own world. As Cousin Morgan would say for years to come, it was the wedding of the century even if only a handful of friends and family attended it.

~

Five Years Later - Patterson Estate

"I have fulfilled the terms of my grandfather's will," Elaine Patterson stood in her father's study. "So I want what is rightfully mine," she demanded. No one looking at the thirty-five-year-old woman could tell that she had just given birth early that morning. "I have provided this estate with the much yearned for heir, and as far as I'm concerned my duty in that respect is now over and done with forever. Now give me what belongs to me."

"Elaine, my child, what changed you from a sweet young woman to this bitter and manipulative creature standing before me right now?" Her father's brow was creased with concern. "Given what you've been through in the past few hours, shouldn't you be resting to regain strength? There's a time for everything, Child."

Elaine scowled at her father. "Papa, there's no need for emotional sentiments. Five years ago, you threatened that if I didn't get married then my inheritance would go to my imbecile cousin, Roger." She shuddered and grimaced with distaste as she thought about her cousin who was always hopeful of taking over the inheritance from her. Not if she could help it! She had sacrificed her life for this estate, and no one was going to snatch this victory from her. "So, I found a simpleton of a man who wouldn't be any trouble to me at all and married him. Then you said that I could only get the inheritance if I provided the estate with an heir. And much as it displeased me, I had to endure much unpleasantness to make that happen. I did what you asked and now it's time for you to fulfil your own end of the agreement."

"Won't you even at least let me go and take a look at my grandson," her elderly father slowly rose to his feet. "Please allow me to go and see my dear grandson. Then we can talk about anything else after that."

"Pa, the boy is a normal child. He has ten fingers and ten toes, if that's what you want to count. My simpleton of a husband named him Herbert, a weak name if you ask me, and I just hope that the child won't take after his worthless father."

Mr. Patterson shook his head at his daughter's words. Every father hoped to have a daughter who was gentle and tender hearted, but that wasn't the case with his only child. Though he loved Elaine very much, he often wondered if all her hardness stemmed from the fact that she'd grown up without a mother. He'd lost his beloved wife when Elaine was six, and his mother had taken over the role of parenting her. Many times, he was filled with regret that he hadn't stepped in occasionally to make sure that she was receiving the kind of care and upbringing suitable for a little girl. For he admitted that his own mother had been a tough woman, not known for her gentleness. Perhaps if his Rose hadn't died so young and so early, she might have steered their beautiful daughter in the right direction.

Now he blamed himself for his daughter turning out this way, a woman who had scoffed at numerous suitable suitors, men of class and worth, unlike the simpleton she'd married. But Mr. Patterson also admitted that he'd pushed his daughter into this situation by insisting that she get married and subsequently produce an heir if she ever wanted to inherit anything, according to her grandfather's will.

"I'm going to take a rest, but this conversation is far from over," Elaine said haughtily, but her father noticed the tired look and shadows under her eyes. Any other noble woman would be lying in bed and accepting all the fuss being made over her after giving birth, but not his Elaine.

She had to prove that she was a strong woman, and he was afraid that her stubbornness would one day be her undoing. Still, he kept his thoughts to himself as he followed her out of the living room.

Expecting her to lead the way to her bedchamber, he was surprised when she headed in the opposite direction, towards the rooms reserved for their guests. Much as he wanted to say something to express his disapproval of the way she conducted her marital life, he decided that this wasn't the time. In any case, he had a grandson to welcome into the family.

"My son," Edwin touched his new-born baby's brow with a careful and gentle hand. "You're the future and I want the best for you," he murmured. Edwin was always very careful to stay out of his wife's way because he couldn't stand being humiliated any more than he already was. Even though he was happy that he now had a son, he felt sad because Elaine and her father had insisted that the child should be named Patterson, bearing his maternal surname. Then he reminded himself that he'd done the same when he'd married Elaine, and his own surname had been pushed out of the way.

Not for the first time Edwin told himself that he'd sold his soul to the devil, and all to keep his mother out of debtors' prison or the workhouse. He didn't once regret the sacrifices he made for his beloved mother, who had died as a free woman two years ago. She'd also died without knowing that he himself was Elaine's captive.

Even though his wife had settled his father's debts immediately after they married, she'd insisted on taking over ownership of their small cottage, and that was what she'd used to keep him subdued. Even after the two years stipulated in their marriage agreement had passed, Elaine had refused to let Edwin go free.

"I won't have you leaving me just so you can go and marry some village girl," she told him contemptuously when he begged for his freedom. "Never will it be said of me that I couldn't keep a husband. I won't be humiliated in that way after all that I've sacrificed," she'd hissed.

"We had an agreement," he protested, but his words fell on deaf ears. "We were to remain married for only two years and then go our separate ways."

"Yes, we did, but if you insist on gaining your freedom from me, then your mother will become homeless, and I'll have her committed to a workhouse."

Her words had shocked him., "Why would you be so cruel when I married you as we agreed? We were to remain in a marriage of convenience for only two years, then I would be free. Why would you go back on our arrangement?"

She'd given him a cold look, "The terms of my grandfather's will state that before I inherit fully, I must provide an heir for this estate, a boy child to take after my father."

"But what if we have a girl?" Edwin asked angrily. He realised that he should have listened to his mother's warning on his wedding day. She'd told him that these people weren't to be trusted but he hadn't listened. "Nothing was ever said about you and me having a child or children together!" He shuddered slightly.

Elaine's eyes narrowed at the expression on her husband's face. "You don't have to look at me with so much contempt and revulsion. Believe me, if there was any other way of having a child without putting up with all that it entails, I would do it. I wouldn't need you and you could then go on your merry way. But we're stuck with each other until I can get what I want. If we have a girl, then we'll have to keep trying until a boy comes along." She shuddered, "Would to God that the first child will be a boy so I have no need of any further torment of intimacy with you or any other man for that matter. But this estate is rightfully mine and I'll do anything to get it, even if it means putting myself through the horrors of childbirth right from the conception part."

That was three years ago, and Edwin recalled what his mother had told him. Her predictions had come true and now he was in a situation from which he couldn't extricate himself. Even though Elaine had promised to set him free after having a child, once again she changed her mind just this morning.

"The boy needs his father," was what she'd told him after the midwife had left. "The child cannot grow up without his father by his side. I know you want to go and marry some village girl. I won't have my son sharing his father with some halfwits birthed by a country bumpkin. No, Edwin, we'll stay married for the rest of our lives if you ever want to see this boy again. Try to leave me, and you'll never know any peace in your life. My son will not grow up being called a half sibling to some lowlife halfwits running around in this village. I won't have my son growing up knowing that his father is married to someone else."

That's when Edwin resigned himself to the reality that he was stuck in this marriage for the rest of his life. Much as it filled him with dismay, he drew comfort from the fact that this child was a boy, and he wouldn't have to endure any more false intimacy with his wife. He had a son whom he already loved deeply, and he was determined to be the buffer between his wife and the child. There was no way he was going to allow his child to become as cold and heartless as his mother.

Footsteps coming down the corridor alerted him to the fact that someone would soon be joining him, and he quickly rose to his feet, for he'd been kneeling beside his son's bassinet, and waited. Expecting it to be his wife, he was surprised that it was his father-in-law who entered the bed chamber. Not desiring to get into any conflict with his wife's father, Edwin prepared himself to leave the room.

"No, stay," he was told in a gentle voice. "I only came to see the child." Edwin was surprised that his father-in-law was even talking to him. In the five years that he and Elaine had been married, the two of them had barely exchanged more than a couple of words at a time.

Edwin knew that his father-in-law despised him and thought of him as nothing but an opportunist and a gold digger. He agreed within himself that he deserved all the scorn heaped upon his head. His wife said he was weak and spineless, and he'd never once refuted her claims upon his character. A stronger man would have walked away long time ago, indeed one full of strength would never have entered into an agreement such as he had.

He watched silently as his father-in-law slowly drew closer to the bassinet. It shocked him to see that the man was growing frailer with each passing day, and with each passing day, he seemed less formidable. It was as if the man knew that his end was nigh and so was making peace all around him.

"The child will grow up to be a very handsome boy," Mr Patterson said as he stood over the bassinet and looked down at his sleeping grandson. "I just pray that he becomes a man of strength and character too." The wistful tone surprised Edwin, but he said nothing. "If only there was time…" The man let his words trail away, and Edwin felt compassion within his heart. It was clear that Mr. Patterson didn't have many months to live.

"I'm sorry," the younger man found himself saying.

Mr. Patterson gave him a lopsided smile, probably the first since they'd known each other. "Don't be. You've done a fine thing, and I thank you."

Then, as if realising whom he was talking to, Mr. Patterson walked to the door and paused without turning around. "You know that you can never leave now," the man said in a soft voice. "Who else will guide this child into being the kind of man you want him to be, a man full of understanding but also compassion? It saddens me to say this, but if you left your son in the upkeep of his mother, you'll only ever have yourself to blame should he turn out to be as cold and manipulative as she is. Think about that." With those words, Mr. Patterson walked out of the room.

Edwin silently agreed, because he could never leave his son at the mercy of his cold wife. For as long as he lived, he would always be there to guide his son.

Ravenscroft Pembroke Wales

Their little cottage was a small stone building which had been part of a larger estate that was now nothing more than a ruin. Five years had gone by since their small but beautiful wedding, and their love for each other grew stronger with each passing day.

On this particular day, Clive and Ashley Chester sat on the old sofa, arms around each other. She was trembling and he held her close, feeling her pain and wanting to say something but lacking the words with which to comfort his distraught wife.

"Five years," Ashley was murmuring tearfully. "When will it be our turn to celebrate?" Her voice caught on a sob. "All our friends and family who got married after us have two and some even three children by now." She looked down at her hands. "My arms feel so empty."

The brokenness in her voice made Clive want to cry, but he had to be strong for her because she needed him. If he broke down now, then what would happen to his Ash? "My love, we'll have children, all in good time. The Lord will hear our cry and bless us with children."

"My arms long to hold a baby in them. Now the women in the village are calling me barren and dry wood, an empty vessel." She sniffed as the tears rolled down her cheeks. "Everyone refers to me as the woman who cannot have children for her husband, and I can't take it anymore," Ashley sobbed. "What good is a woman who can't bear children for her husband?"

Clive was angry that the people he'd grown up amongst could be this cruel to the one he loved. "Ignore them, for they know not what they say. Children are a gift from the

Lord, and He'll give us ours in His own good time. I promise you that the children we have will be very special, and this wait will be worth it."

Ashley refused to be comforted, and she pulled away from her husband. "I would have remained silent and not complained about anything," she wiped her face. "But now your father has also started saying that he's sorry he allowed you and me to get married. Father Chester has always been on my side, but it seems as if even he is tired of waiting for a grandchild. You should put me aside and take a woman who will bear children for you. Father Chester says his lineage has to continue, and it seems as if I'm the one stopping that from happening. I can't have that on my conscience," She covered her face with her palms.

"Perish the thought," Clive said strongly. "Children are a blessing from the Lord, as I said, and He will give them to us in His own good time. I don't want you to think about any of the nasty things people are saying because I love you with or without children. I never married you for your childbearing abilities but because you were given to me by the Lord Himself. Ash, you and I are destined to be together for the rest of our lives, and nothing will ever make me leave you. My promise to you stands stronger today than it was on the day we first met. Nothing on earth will ever make me leave you, because I love you so much. You're my life, my heart, and my home, Ash. Please don't ever ask me to leave you, for you'll be breaking my heart."

Ashley smiled through her tears even though her heart was still heavy. She longed for a child but didn't want to cause distress to her husband with further talk on the matter. She knew that Clive loved her and would do anything to make her happy, including taking her side very strongly against those who spoke ill of her.

Yet their relatives wouldn't leave them alone. After two years of marriage with no issue in sight, they had started dropping subtle hints here and there which she'd chosen to ignore. But now five years later and they were openly and blatantly coming out to ask her when she would provide her husband with a child, but they did this, of course, whenever Clive wasn't present. All subtlety and diplomacy were gone, and whenever any of them got the chance, they asked her what she was still waiting for and why she wasn't a mother yet. They would then compare her to her peers who already had children. Things were now so bad that she'd started thinking of a way that she would leave Ravenscroft.

She loved Clive dearly, and the thought of leaving him was like a deep wound in her heart, but he was also suffering due to their childlessness, and he deserved better. Maybe if she left, then Clive would eventually be free to marry a woman who could give him children and carry on his family name. She was tired of being mocked and ridiculed and treated as a pariah. Even her own relatives had joined those who taunted and made unkind remarks. The only one who stood by her was Cousin Morgan. Their mothers, both long dead, had been sisters, and even though there was an age gap of nearly ten years between the two cousins, they were very close.

Their friendship had been made stronger because it was through Cousin Morgan that Ashley had met Clive. He'd come to her house to clean her chimney. Ashley was visiting on that day and the rest had been history. Cousin Morgan had encouraged their relationship, and when they finally married, she'd even provided a room for them in her small cottage until they were able to find their own place. Over the years, it was Cousin Morgan who had held Ashley and comforted her when the unkind remarks became too much for her to bear.

That's why two days later when Clive left the house to go to work at the fish store Ashley made her way to her cousin's place. She shared her grief with her relative and friend, knowing that she would receive much needed comforting and she wasn't disappointed. It was close to lunch time, and as they prepared a simple meal of mashed potatoes and broth from boiled bones, Morgan shared words of comfort to her distraught cousin.

"The more you listen to all those tattlers, the more distressed you'll get," Cousin Morgan told her. She'd been married at the age of sixteen, but her husband died two years later, leaving her childless. She'd remained a widow and refused to remarry, even though she had a number of offers over the years, for she was still a beautiful woman even at the age of thirty-five. "When I refused to remarry after my Simon's death, the same people accused me of all manner of things. Woe unto me if I was ever caught standing with someone's husband or even just exchanging greetings with them. They called me all manner of names, but since I knew that I wasn't what they termed me to be, I simply chose to live my life and ignored them. Eventually they learnt to leave me alone, and now in my old age, nobody bothers about me again," she chuckled.

"Cousin Morgan, you're not at all old. There's still so much life left in you, and if I may say so, you'll probably outlive all of us. Even now I know that a few gentlemen wouldn't hesitate to take you as their wife, if you would only give them the chance."

"Why Ashley, you're so kind to say that," the older woman grinned. "That's why I'm telling you to shut your ears to what these people are saying. Ignore them and they'll soon learn to leave you alone. The more you show them that their words are hurtful and wounding you, the more they'll continue talking about you."

When Ashley left her cousin's house, her steps were lighter. She purposed to take Cousin Morgan's advice, and no matter how much ridicule she faced in the coming days, she never said a bad word about anybody. She could see that her new attitude pleased her husband, for she no longer cried or gave in to bouts of depression. This went on for weeks, and Clive was happy that his wife was no longer the miserable and pathetic creature that people's unkind words had tried to turn her into.

Ashley took pleasure in her occupation as a seamstress, and when another of her many cousins decided to get married, she was called upon to adjust the family wedding gown. As she tucked in the delicate fabric, one of the pearl buttons came loose and fell off the dress. It rolled under the chair, and as she was trying to reach for it, Imogen arrived to pick the dress up.

"I'm afraid one of the buttons has fallen off," Ashley told Imogen. "It rolled under the chair, and I was just about to search for it when you arrived."

"Don't worry about it," Imogen said hurriedly, looking quite flustered. "Just give me the dress, and I'll bring it back once my wedding is over."

"Which reminds me, you haven't told me what I can do to help. Now that your wedding is in a month's time, how can I be of assistance to you?"

Imogen shrugged, "You might as well know because it will soon be all over the village." She was a pretty girl with wide brown eyes and thick dark hair. "I'm in the family way, so Henry said that we should go to Gretna Green because the old minister refused to wed us. We made a mistake." She looked miserable. "But I don't want my child born out of wedlock, so we'll go to Gretna Green and get married there. Henry is waiting for me, and I don't have time anymore. Just give me the dress."

Ashley packed the dress as best as she could, telling Imogen to be very careful because the fabric was now very delicate. It hadn't been used since Ashley's own wedding, because the other brides in the family had chosen to get newer ones, but her cousin wanted to get away as fast as she could and merely waved the caution aside. Once she was gone, Ashley sat down at her table and sighed. Even Imogen, five years younger than her, was already with child irrespective of the circumstances of conception. Would she ever hold a baby in her arms? Her hand went to her flat stomach, and she sighed once again.

"Dear Lord, You give children in Your own good time. Please grant my husband and me the blessing of a little one and take my shame away. Please, Lord."

When she heard the heavy tread on the doorstep, she knew that her husband was back. Quickly schooling her features into a smile, she bent down to search for the missing pearl button. She would put it on a string around her neck until Imogen returned the wedding gown and then she would sew it back. Finding it, she did just that as the door opened and her husband entered the house.

"What are you doing down on your knees on the cold floor?" He placed his satchel and a small package on the table.

"Cousin Imogen was just here." She told him everything. "I was searching for this button." She raised the string that was around her neck and on which the pearl button now rested. "I don't want to lose it, so I've made a necklace out of it. When Imogen returns the dress, I'll sew it back on. I just hope she doesn't tear that gown up in her haste."

"That lucky button is safely resting in the right place," her husband cheered. "Well, won't you give your tired husband his usual kiss to welcome him home?" The cheeky look in his eyes made her blush.

Ashley might have continued to persevere the ill treatment meted out by her relatives on both sides and also ignore unkind remarks tossed her way, but for something that happened to shake her to the roots of her heart.

Mrs. Burns' niece came to visit her, and the girl decided that she wanted Clive by any means necessary. Clive was a decent and morally upright man who loved his wife and respected his employer, but Stacy Brim was a spoilt young woman and a real troublemaker.

A few days after her arrival in Ravenscroft, Stacy came to the cottage when Clive was at the shop. Ashley had just finished cleaning the house when she heard a knock at the door. Even though their cottage was one of many still standing on the dilapidated estate, Ashley was always careful to keep her door locked securely especially when she was all alone in the house. Her nearest neighbour was just a few feet away, but Ash felt safer behind locked doors. The only time she ever left the door unlocked was when her husband was at home with her. The knock came again, and the person sounded rather impatient.

"Who is it?" she asked when the knocking persisted. She was sure that it wasn't Cousin Morgan, for her relative was visiting friends in Cardiff and wasn't expected back for another few days. Nor was it Clive, for he had his own key. "Who is it?" she asked again, not intending to open the door for any strangers.

"Mrs. Chester, my name is Stacy, and Mrs. Burns is my aunt. I've come to see you because I feel that we need to have a woman-to-woman discussion."

Ashley wondered why Mrs. Burns' niece was here and what she wanted. She barely knew the young lady, but out of curiosity she decided to open the door a fraction. She wasn't willing to let the other woman into her home because they weren't friends, and she didn't know what she wanted. And besides that, Ashley didn't have time for idle chatter and gossip because she was busy with her chores.

"I'm surprised that you would come to my house," she said, only part of her face visible to the visitor. "How may I help you?"

"Won't you let me in?" Stacy looked taken aback at the lack of welcome.

Ash shook her head. "You caught me in the middle of doing some thorough cleaning and I'm rather busy. I don't have time to spend chatting. My husband will soon be home, and I don't want him to find the house dirty and his dinner not prepared."

Stacy laughed, an unkind sound. "I just wanted to see for myself the kind of worthless woman that has refused to grant Clive his freedom. Do you know that he loves me?"

"You're lying." Ash didn't want to listen to anymore falsehoods because she knew that there was no way Clive could ever be unfaithful to her. He was too honourable a man to do that. She tried to shut the door, but Stacy put a foot in the doorway and blocked her attempt.

"Am I?" Stacy answered sassily. "When your husband gets home today, why don't you ask him where he was last evening? Didn't he come home very late?"

Ash frowned, wondering what the woman was getting at. Clive sometimes arrived home late when he was waiting to purchase fish from the trawlers. "I know that he was at the pier getting fish from the trawlers, just as he always does."

Stacy threw her head back and laughed, "Well if that's what you want to believe then so be it. But if I were you, I would insist on finding out where the man was, and you might be surprised at the answer."

With those words hanging in the air, Stacy turned her back and walked away, leaving Ash with many questions in her mind. She didn't want to believe that her husband could have been anywhere other than the place that he was supposed to be, but would Stacy Brim have made the journey to her house just to tell her false news? No, something must have happened for the woman to be so bold as to come out here and mock her. Ashley was determined that she would get to the truth, come what may!

Continue reading this unforgettable Christmas saga...

Read Orphan Christmas Miracle on Amazon

OUR GIFT TO YOU

AS A WAY TO SAY THANK YOU WE WOULD LOVE TO SEND YOU THIS BEAUTIFUL STORY FREE OF CHARGE.

Click here for your free copy of Whitechapel Waif

PureRead.com/victorian

At PureRead we publish books you can trust. Great tales without smut or swearing, but with all of the mystery and romance you expect from a great story.

Be the first to know when we release new books, take part in our fun competitions, and get surprise free books in your inbox by signing up to our free VIP Reader list.

As a welcome gift you'll receive the story of the Whitechapel Waif straight to your inbox...

Click here for your free copy of Whitechapel Waif

PureRead.com/victorian

OUR GIFT TO YOU

AS A WAY TO SAY THANK YOU WE WOULD LOVE TO SEND YOU THIS BEAUTIFUL STORY FREE OF CHARGE.

Click here for your free copy of Whitechapel Waif

PureRead.com/victorian

At PureRead we publish books you can trust. Great tales without smut or swearing, but with all of the mystery and romance you expect from a great story.

Be the first to know when we release new books, take part in our fun competitions, and get surprise free books in your inbox by signing up to our free VIP Reader list.

As a welcome gift you'll receive the story of the Whitechapel Waif straight to your inbox...

Click here for your free copy of Whitechapel Waif

PureRead.com/victorian